"AFTER YOU, HOLMES..."

Four pastiches

by

Douglas Moreton

With original photographs from the collection of

John H Watson, M.D.

Ian Henry Publications

ISBN 0 86025 287 6

Ian Henry Publications, Ltd.
20 Park Drive, Romford, Essex RM1 4LH

Simultaneously published in Australia, Canada, U.K., and U.S.A.

Printed by
Interprint, Ltd.
Malta

Introduction

In the stories - four long and fifty-six short - presented to the public through my great-grandfather's late literary agent, Arthur Conan Doyle, it would appear that Mr Sherlock Holmes's celebrated cases did not range north beyond the Peak District of Derbyshire.

It can only be assumed that, as Conan Doyle as a boy boarded first at Hodder, the preparatory school for Stonyhurst College, and then at Stonyhurst itself, arguably the most prestigious Roman Catholic school in England, he suppressed such stories in some mistaken belief that he should protect that part of England from the scandal of being investigated by the world's first consulting detective.

This is even more strange when one considers that Stonyhurst is the repository of such priceless relics as the cloak worn by Henry VIII at the Field of the Cloth of Gold, and the jewelled Book of Hours that Mary, Queen of Scots, carried to the execution block, and lies athwart the two great dominances of the region: the Forest of Bowland, reaching up as far as the Roman city of Lancaster, and Pendle Hill, one-time haunt of the Pendle Witches.

Stuff here - and more - for a hundred tales; the four in this volume show that my great-grandfather and his friend did, in fact, exchange the crepuscular fog of London for the creeping mists of those fell-girt places that had played host to their literary agent.

Two of them - *The Case of the Counterfeit Corpse* and *Coffins at Candlemas* - are set within the eastern hundreds of the County Palatine of Lancaster. Thence we journey into the then West Riding of Yorkshire, there to encounter *The Case of the Missing Masters*, a chronicle of false pride and avarice set in the ancient city of Ripon. And so, by convolute passage to Crick, in the pastoral quietude of Shropshire, where Holmes and Watson are faced with *The Case of the Singular Sibling.*

What makes this collection even more interesting is that, among the pages of the manuscript that was recovered from a vault in Coutts & Co. Bank were a number of photographs and sketches. Which of these were taken by Dr Watson himself and which he acquired from other sources and added them to the documents to add local colour is unclear, but some of them are reproduced here, necessarily uncredited.

Gareth Footage-Watson

The Case of the Counterfeit Corpse

Certain of the cases to come the way of my friend and colleague Mr Sherlock Holmes during his career as a consulting detective were, for one reason or another, deemed by him unsuitable for the public record. Exceptionally, he would come to see a particular case in another light and would rescind the disqualification, and when this happened I was privileged to chronicle to the best of my ability the facts of the matter.

A fascinating example concerns the singular conduct of a Minister of the Crown, in which instance Holmes suppressed the details for ten years, and then sanctioned their publication on the understanding that I should by means of a false name protect the individual's identity and leave unspecified where the consequence of his folly resulted.

Suffice to say, therefore, that the events I am about to describe unfolded sometime during that span of years when political power in Britain alternated between the Tories, under Lord Salisbury, and the Liberal Party, led by Mr William Ewart Gladstone; and when, more pertinently, the outcome of an impending General Election promised to be so finely balanced that an unprecedented number of Members of Parliament were, perforce, forsaking the whirl of Westminster for the backwaters of their constituencies.

Not least among these was a prominent Cabinet Minister and Member of the Privy Council, who, notwithstanding his high office, found both his seat and his portfolio hostage to the provincial vox populi he had failed to notice since last he canvassed it.

The introduction of Mr Sherlock Homes into the affairs of this perfunctory politician came about one morning, when the door to our sitting-room burst open and Billy ushered in a burly, fresh-faced individual who attempted the removal of a brown bowler hat at one and the same time as he contrived to throw back the cape of a travel-creased Inverness.

"I am Mister Tobias Cobb," announced he, in a powerful baritone. "Arrived at Baker Street on a matter of the utmost gravity."

"Dear me," murmured Holmes, not troubling to rise from his side of the fire. "Grave for whom, pray?"

"For Justice!" thundered the other, clasping to his breast the hollow of his hat. "For Truth and Fair Play!"

My reaction to these histrionics was that they would unleash that side of my friend's tongue that can so swiftly deflate a poseur but instead I perceived in Holmes a certain languid tolerance of the situation. Then, to my greater surprise and interest, he dismissed the Buttons and embarked upon one of those masterly deductive dissertations for which he is justly famous.

"Your incognito is frail," he began, "for it is obvious to me that you are a representative of the official police."

"I will not deny it."

"Here on official business."

"Yes."

"But not officially."

"You read much into an omission of rank, Mr Holmes."

"Oh, pooh, pooh!" Holmes waved a disclaimer, then joined his hands and regarded the policeman over steepled fingers. "That was but one link in the chain of observation and deduction." And when the bushy eyebrows opposite rose towards the thatch of corn-coloured hair: "Doctor Watson here knows my methods and, like me, had doubtless already concluded from your dress and bearing that you are what you are. The lack of official standing is retrospectively confirmed by the significantly short interval between the arrival of your conveyance and the pull at our bell."

"Which suggests nothing."

"On the contrary, it suggests that having paid off the cabby you made no record of the transaction, which in turn suggests that the journey was made at your own expense."

Following this most succinct of explanations, I witnessed in the demeanour of our visitor a most profound change. In a trice his offensive brashness seemed to fall from him, leaving in its stead an honest simplicity of purpose that I found not unappealing.

"You are correct in every particular," he confessed, sinking heavily into the chair indicated to him. "You will be saying next that I am not a Scotland Yarder, and that I hail from the back of beyond."

"Oh, come now," smiled Sherlock Holmes, "I should hardly be so ungracious as to describe the County Palatine of Lancaster in those terms. But pray do not continue to appear so astonished, for your speech, if I may say so, is characteristic of the region. Indeed, I would go so far as to surmise that you are the North Country official mentioned in a recent column of The *Times*. Make a long arm, Watson there's a good fellow, and hand down that third volume."

Opening the large scrap-book that I presented, Mr Sherlock Holmes lapsed into a busy silence baffled no doubt by the eclecticism of his filing habits. Eventually, however, he found what he sought and commenced reading aloud. "'The Rt. Hon. Treasure Fortune, M.P., (¹) who last week collapsed while the guest of honour at a civic reception at B------ Town Hall, has since returned to Westminster, where he is reported as fully recovered and discharging his ministerial duties. A local physician who attended the statesman immediately following his indisposition has denied that his patient's condition at any time gave cause for more than passing concern. A sergeant of police who was called to the scene has made a full report as to the circumstances, and it is understood that no official action of any sort is contemplated. A spokesman for the Chief Constable stated categorically that the sergeant was entirely satisfied with the outcome of his inquiries, and was presently engaged in duties of another kind'. Well?" rapped Holmes, clapping shut the book. "Am I not right?"

"As right as that stuff is nine parts false, Mr Holmes!"

"Strong words, Mr Cobb."

"Strong and true, Mr Holmes."

"Well, well, we shall see. Pray be precise as to details."

"I'll be that all right! When I saw this Treasure Fortune, he wasn't ill, Mr Sherlock Holmes - he was dead!

"I may not be a medical man, Doctor Watson," he continued, turning to me, "but I've seen many a corpse in my job, and this was another. There wasn't the flutter of a pulse against my fingers or a whisper of breath on the mirror I put to his face. He was dead, I tell you! As dead as mutton!"

Throughout this remarkable interlude Holmes sat like a man transfixed. In all the years we have been together I have rarely seen him so absorbed, and I was pondering how best to penetrate the mood, when its creator startled us afresh.

"As for being satisfied with the treatment of my report, the only satisfaction I have is knowing that every word is true. That means more to me than the promotion I received."

"You are to be congratulated on your integrity," commented Holmes, coming out of his brown study. "And on your advancement."

"Oh, an inspectorship is all very grand, but when the task that accompanies it entails being shut up at the very top of the station, with nothing better to do than compile lists relating to the stabling of police horses..."

"At the top of the building, you say?" interrupted Holmes, leaping to his feet, as if by this action he might somehow join his informant at that elevation. "Entirely alone?"

"With only a cat for company!"

"Who did this work before?"

"No one."

"From when, exactly, did it take effect?"

"From the day after I submitted my report on Mr Treasure Fortune - the same day my superiors confiscated my pocket-book and kicked me upstairs."

"By Jove, Watson!" cried Sherlock Holmes, commencing to pace to-and-fro, "I am beginning to see daylight. It is my experience of hierarchies that those they would stifle they invariably promote to positions of absolute inconsequence. And in this instance, of virtual isolation.

"Has anyone beyond this room knowledge of your presence here?" he demanded earnestly of Tobias Cobb. And when the other denied the possibility: "Capital! On no account compromise that situation, for this promises to be a most sinister business. One false step could see us plunged into the abyss. But let us consult the *Bradshaw*. I believe there is an express train to Manchester at five minutes after twelve o'clock ..." (^{2})

The tedium of our long journey north was made tolerable by our good fortune in securing to ourselves a first-class smoking-compartment, and by the resumption of our client's recollections.

"Tell me about Mr Treasure Fortune's dinner companions," invited Holmes, at one point. "Who sat on either side of him at the commencement of the meal?"

"His Worship the Mayor, Sir Malacaster Kark, was on his left, with the Town Clerk, Mr Armitage Lamb, on his right."

"I see. And at what stage of the proceedings did their guest become unwell?"

"During the first course."

"Which consisted of?"

"A handful of small black objects."

"Ha! Caviar, I fancy - the pickled row of the sturgeon. Excellent! Excellent!" Holmes fairly radiated approbation. "Not only did our friend take note of the delicacy, Watson, he accurately describes it. Let us hope that his small talent for observation was not the prisoner of an aspiring palate but encompassed events at large. Well, Mr Cobb?"

"Well, sir, if it's all the same to you, I should like to say how I came to be on the premises in the first place."

Following which rejoinder, Tobias Cobb's tone took on that stolid, strung-together quality peculiar to members of the official police when giving evidence. It seems that immediately after the first course was served, there occurred a commotion in the main entrance to the banqueting hall, where an intruder dressed in a sandwich-board forced his way in. According to Cobb, the pandemonium that ensued was not so much on account of the trespass as the offensive nature of the Bolshevist slogans daubed on the placards.

"The door through which the fellow entered?" interpolated Holmes. "Does it face the top table?" And when Cobb assented: "And is it approximately opposite where the guest of honour was seated? Just so! Now I urge you to consider before answering my next question, for I have a notion that the bizarre happenings about which you complain may hinge upon it."

It was typical of Mr Sherlock Holmes that having set the stage he did not at once ring up the curtain, and for the time being there was no sound save that of our breathing and the muffled thrum of the carriage wheels over the metals beneath our feet. Beyond the windows of the compartment the mighty brick-clad octopus that is present-day London - and along one of whose tapering tentacles we yet sped - was reluctantly disgorging snatches of open country, and as our silence lengthened I surrendered my gaze to that strange duality of perception wherein objects in the foreground appear to race past at great speed, while those in the distance give the impression of travelling majestically in the same direction as the beholder.

It was while my attention was thus diverted that Holmes inquired of Cobb what direction the sandwich-board man took upon entering the banqueting hall.

"Why, to the left, Mr Holmes."

"But to whose left, Mr Cobb? Did he turn to his own left, or to the left of those regarding him from in front?"

"Upon gaining access the gate-crasher turned to his left,

that is, to the right of the three seated at the top table. It is my opinion that he intended to make a circuit of the hall."

"But he did not do so?"

"No. He had paraded some few paces when Sir Malacaster Kark pointed to where the man was and ordered his removal, which was effected by a police constable. I myself remained on the premises in case of need."

"Which soon turned out to be the case, did it not?"

"Yes. Only minutes later the principal guest became prostrate."

"What was the singularity of his condition?"

"The singularity, Mr Holmes?"

"Just so. Someone who has been strangled to death does not exhibit a bullet wound!"

"Well, there was nothing like that, of course, but I did notice that his face was exceptionally pink."

"Did you perceive anything else?"

"That there was a bitter smell on his lips, and that he was experiencing great difficulty in breathing."

"What steps did you take to alleviate his suffering?"

"Sir Malacaster Kark and Mr Armitage Lamb assisted me in transporting the gentleman to an annexe, where there was a couch, and where we were joined shortly by Doctor Marriot Jaymes."

"What opinion did the medico vouchsafe?"

"That the fellow was dead, Mr Holmes - a conclusion I had already arrived at."

"To what did he attribute the cause of death?"

"To apoplexy."

"And the aroma you mentioned?"

"To an aperitif containing angostura bitters."

"And were you satisfied with this diagnosis?"

"I had no reason to be otherwise. Doctor Marriot Jaymes runs a private nursing home specializing in such disorders. In point of fact, Sir Malacaster Kark had until the day of the function been undergoing treatment there."

Manchester London Road Station; the busy concourse that greeted
Holmes and his companions at about 4.20 that afternoon

"And how does the good doctor explain Mr Treasure Fortune's revivification?"

"As to that, I cannot say, Mr Holmes, for I have had no contact with him since the evening of the tragedy. Twenty-four hours later the matter was taken out of my hands, and it was made pretty plain by my superiors that should I pursue it in any way I would imperil both my position and my pension."

Holmes digested what he had learned in a prolonged bout of silence, chin sunk almost on the top button of his waistcoat. Only someone who knew him as well as I could appreciate that within that still, down-thrust head a matchless reasoning faculty was functioning with all the power and precision of a finely-tuned racing engine. The elements of the problem were its motive source and the thrill of the chase its lubricant. For the time being the shell that housed the engine was in repose, but I knew that at the right moment the entire machine would leap into action.

Suddenly our train plunged into a tunnel through which we rattled and roared in utter darkness. When at last we emerged, Holmes stirred himself sufficiently to say: "At this rate we shall soon be arrived in Manchester. Let us hope that our onward journey will not be by means of a parliamentary train (³), for I shall begrudge each second that its passage delays my interrogation of the man who spoke so loudly that he went unnoticed."

And with this enigmatic remark, Mr Sherlock Holmes leaned back and closed his eyes.

***

"Well, Watson," observed my friend over breakfast the next morning, "had it been possible to break a vial of amyl nitrite under the patient's nose his life might have been saved."

"I am not aware that amyl nitrite is indicated in cases of cerebral haemorrhage, Holmes."

"Nor is it."

`... by way of a busy main road flanked on either side by a variety of small shops and businesses...'

"Then wherein lies its efficacy in this instance?"

"As an antidote following the administration of potassium cyanide."

"Steady on, Holmes! it is one thing to suggest that the demise of a public figure has in some way been concealed, but to suppose poison ..."

"I do not suppose anything. It is a matter of fact. I am likewise certain that murder has been done."

"Good Lord! But how was the narcotic introduced? Ha! The aperitif!"

"I think not, Watson. The smell of angostura bitters is piquant rather than bitter (4). Now if you are finished your eggs and bacon, we will pay a call upon Mr Armitage Lamb."

The posting house where Tobias Cobb had lodged us lay within easy walking distance of the Town Hall, and our mid-morning excursion took us there by way of a busy main road flanked on either side by a variety of small shops and businesses. It was as we waited at the curbside preparatory to crossing the road that there lurched toward us a clanking articulated tramcar, the leading element of which emitted from its stack black clouds of evil-smelling smoke.

I was reminded of this intimidating encounter some ten minutes later, when Holmes made adroit use of it informally to open an interview he clearly regarded as crucial to our investigation.

"Yes, our `steamers' are somewhat daunting," agreed Mr Armitage Lamb, when we were seated. "Not unlike the Ironclads they are said to resemble. But come, Mr Holmes, you are not here to try conclusions (5) with our `Baltic Fleet'!"

"No indeed," replied Holmes, smiling. "I am come with the intention of reaching an altogether different conclusion. I am anxious to meet the master of ceremonies who officiated at the function attended by yourself and Mr Treasure Fortune."

`... there lurched toward us a clanking articulated tramcar...'

The pause that followed this statement was eloquent of the sense of anticlimax it evoked. "That will be Kirby," the Town Clerk said, finally. "Though I cannot conceive in what manner he can assist you. "

"What is his regular occupation?"

"He is employed in my department as a trusted messenger."

"And his ceremonial duties?"

"Are performed as and when required."

"A somewhat unusual combination, is it not?"

"Kirby is an unusual type of man. He is a self-taught former non-commissioned officer - a sergeant, I believe - who has turned a natural bent into a public service. But I will have him in so that you may question him personally."

"You are most kind. Perhaps while we are waiting I might inquire how you reacted to the news that Mr Treasure Fortune had returned from the dead?"

"I was delighted, naturally."

"But not incredulous?"

"Incredulity is first cousin to disbelief, Mr Holmes."

"Quite so."

"Then my answer is in the negative. When a medical man of Doctor Jaymes's standing admits to having made a mistake and declares that his patient is miraculously recovered, one does not question the outcome."

"When did he inform you of this?"

"The same day that the Government people arrived and took charge, that is the day after the evening when the Minister was pronounced dead."

"What more did he divulge?"

"That Mr Treasure Fortune and his companions were returning to London."

"By what means did they travel?"

"The railway authorities placed a special train at their disposal I understand that it pulled out of a closed platform at one minute to midnight."

"There's another matter that interests me," remarked Holmes. "I have it that Sir Malacaster Kark was until recently a patient in Dr Jaymes's private nursing home?"

"And is so again, Mr Holmes. He returned to Aspen House the same night there was such turmoil at the reception. I am afraid the strain was too much for him."

"Yet he felt well enough to attend?"

"He felt that it was his duty to do so. You see, he and Mr Treasure Fortune were at school together."

"Had they not met since?"

"Apparently not. When the latter was here campaigning for the last election, Sir Malacaster was elsewhere - he is a mill owner, you know - and prior to that opportunity their paths had not crossed.

My friend regarded Mr Armitage Lamb with great intensity, as if measuring the other's shrewd intelligence. "You are very well informed, Sir."

"Ours is a close-knit community, Mr Holmes. There is little that transpires that does not soon become general knowledge."

"And very little general knowledge that does not contain its own closely guarded secret," murmured Holmes. "But this must be Sergeant Kirby," he went on, briskly rising to confront a tall, soldierly-looking man, with carefully barbered side-whiskers.

As we had been given to believe, Kirby was atypical of his class, and proved to be a most articulate and well-spoken individual who, when his superior had made known the purpose of the interview, also revealed himself to be a forthcoming and respectful one.

"You are an observant man, I take it?" commenced Sherlock Holmes.

"I think so, Sir."

"With a good memory?"

"Yes, Sir."

"Very well, let us put matters to the test. I wish you to

'... an intruder dressed in a sandwich-board forced his way in...' A common sight, unlikely to attracted premature suspicion.

focus your thoughts on the recent unfortunate events at the Town Hall, and tell me how many public announcements you had made before the proceedings came to a halt."

"Just one, Sir - when I announced dinner."

"In the normal way there would have been more?"

"Oh yes, Sir. I should have announced each speaker, and called out the toasts."

"In anticipation of which procedure you stood where?"

"Behind Sir Malacaster Kark and the guest of honour."

"So it might be said, might it not, that you had an unrivalled view of what happened between everyone sitting down for dinner and its premature conclusion? Please be so kind as to describe the scene."

"Well, sir, the first course had just come up from the galley, when the arrival of a man in a sandwich-board caused a disturbance on the far side of the room. After that, Sir, if you'll allow the comparison, it was like siting a target down the barrel of a rifle, for as soon as Sir Malacaster spotted the source of the trouble he flung out an arm in that direction."

"In short, he pointed an accusing finger? With which hand?"

"His right. I particularly noticed Sir Malacaster's ring when the light caught it."

"Excellent, Kirby, your memory is all that you claim for it. By the by, I was aware that you are an ex-sergeant, but I was not told that you were a sergeant of marines."

"It is a distinction people are apt to forget, Sir," responded Kirby, standing even straighter. "But if you were not correctly informed, Mr Holmes, may I know how you deduced the error?"

Holmes laughed delightedly, obviously willing to indulge an exceptional witness. "To the best of my knowledge, there are two bodies of men who refer to the kitchen as a galley; one lot are sailors. You were not a sailor."

"You have a sharp ear, Sir."

"I am banking upon yours being as sharp. Sharp enough

to hear the table talk between Sir Malacaster Kark and Mr Treasure Fortune. I am postulating a probability, Kirby, not accusing you of eavesdropping."

"If you put it like that, Sir."

"I do. I also put it to you that you can recall the gist of their conversation. In short, Kirby, I wish to know what the two men talked about!"

"They exchanged schoolboy reminiscences, Sir. It was their sole topic.

"Was it a lively interlude?"

"Oh no, Mr Holmes, a very tame business."

"And did their recollections coincide?"

"Invariably."

"Thank you, Kirby, that is most illuminating. I think it may safely be said that what you have told me adds substance to an hypothesis I had already largely developed. Pray do not disturb yourself, Mr Lamb, Doctor Watson and I will see ourselves out."

"I say, Holmes," I remarked, when we were in the open and strolling back to our quarters, "if it is as Mr Armitage Lamb reports, our presence here is already broadcast."

"Very likely."

"And is inimical to the interests of our client."

"Tut, tut, Watson, did you think that we could keep our involvement a secret for long? Nevertheless, there is something in what you say. In the short term, Inspector Tobias Cobb's situation will almost certainly be compromised."

"And in the long term?"

"May be made worse."

"Then we shall have failed him."

"My dear fellow, what a cyclops you are! You see entirely without perspective, and then only in the direction you are looking. I on the other hand see each point of the compass simultaneously. For the present, however, I propose to explore only those two that are diametrically opposed.

"If, as you have just now adumbrated, our intervention on Cobb's behalf is to no avail, then he is ruined and I am discredited. At the other end of the needle, if my efforts in his cause are so absolutely successful that I not only show Mr Treasure Fortune to have lain dead but prove by producing his murderer that he was murdered, our friend's rehabilitation and the continuance of my good name is assured. Unfortunately, events seldom follow such a cut-and-dried course.

"By the way," he continued, in quite a different style, "do you remember your schooldays with exactitude?"

"I cannot say that I do, Holmes? But why do you ask?"

"Because according to Sergeant Kirby, Sir Malacaster Kark and Mr Treasure Fortune recollected theirs in unfailing detail."

Following luncheon, I did not again see Mr Sherlock Holmes until a little after eight o'clock in the evening, when he put in a breezy appearance at the hotel after being absent on some scheme of his own.

"Ah, there you are, Watson!" he greeted me, as if it were I who had that moment returned. "If you are prepared to forego a second brandy and to accompany me this instant, I think I can promise you an entertaining diversion."

"Certainly," said I, rising from the dinner table. "But may I know what is in the wind? Is there the prospect of violence?

"Well, there has been one murder already, and the people we are up against play for high stakes."

"In that case I shall bring my revolver."

"Good man! And now, if you are ready, we must make a start. I will recount what is relevant of my day's activities as we ride in the hansom."

What Holmes, no doubt from force of habit, referred to as a hansom turned out to be a sturdy four-wheeler pulled by a pair of thick-set horses, and it was during our journey in it,

`... adopted the extreme measure of commandeering the police office telephone...'

first through gas-lit streets ringing (6) with town noises and then along quiet country roads, that he kept his promise to bring me up to date.

It appears that by posing as a company agent charged with accounting for expenditure to do with unscheduled traffic, Holmes had bluffed the local railway authorities into revealing that the special train chartered for Mr Treasure Fortune had carried in its luggage-van a sealed mortuary shell. Swearing the awed officials to secrecy, Holmes had next so far extended his audacity as to present his true credentials to the area's chief officer of police, and to instruct him to have men posted with orders to detain anyone leaving a certain location after ten o'clock that night. When the Superintendent had demurred, Holmes had adopted the extreme measure of commandeering the police station telephone and speaking privately and at length to a subscriber in London. As a consequence, when one hour later the bell of the police telephone rang in return, the Superintendent was authorized by his Chief Constable to defer to Mr Sherlock Holmes's every request and requirement.

"What I have set in motion cannot now be arrested," said Holmes grimly, as our conveyance sped through the darkness. "If my theories do not hold water, there is he whose fall will be a hundred times greater than my own. Stop here, Cabby! That's right, on this side of the gates. Down you get, Watson! From here on it is Shanks's pony, for if my reconnaissance of this afternoon is sound we have a quarter of a mile yet to go. Off with you, Cabby! This may prove a lengthy business," he added for my benefit.

I was about to say something in reply, when the lights of the turning four-wheeler revealed cut into each of the stone gate-pillars the words ASPEN HOUSE. For some reason the name sent a shiver through me, although I had heard it mentioned but once and had no cause to dread it.

Slipping through the heavy wrought-iron gates, we gained the driveway beyond and started up it. The going became so uneven, however, and the night so devoid of starlight, that soon Holmes had recourse to a dark lantern (7) that he conjured from the folds of his Inverness.

"Stay close, Watson!" he urged, in a whisper. And some minutes later: "Sssh! We are almost there."

Even as he spoke it loomed before us, a black hulk of a place, with a sheer front extending to several storeys. Everywhere was utterly dark and silent and looked uniformly uninviting, but guided by the natural instinct that would have made him a most formidable cat-burglar Holmes moved unerringly towards a conservatory, where he found first an outer and then an inner door that yielded to his skeleton key.

"Take the lantern," he hissed, when we were within, "and be ready to close the shutter at a moment's warning. If I am not misinformed, the patients' quarters are on the first floor."

So saying, he led the way out of the conservatory and into the house proper, and then ascended by way of a wide staircase to a gloomy landing, from whence, via another, shorter, flight of stairs we arrived at the entrance to a narrow passage down one side of which were a succession of closed doors. Slowly, hardly daring to breath, we tip-toed along the passage opening and closing each door in turn. When we thus reached the last, Holmes raised his finger to his lips and inched the door wide, until I, peering over his shoulder, could see beyond.

The feeble light that burned there created as many shadows as it dispelled, and as my own lamp made its contribution the shadows jumped and tumbled like demented acrobats. In the midst of this mad animation there was the contrasting stillness of a hospital bed, and within it - and of so little substance that the bed's white-sheeted flatness was barely disturbed - an ashen-faced travesty of a human being. Even as I took in the scene, there turned from the bed a tall, menacing figure.

"Good evening, Mr Armitage Lamb," said Mr Sherlock Holmes, stepping boldly forward. "It seems that I have arrived just in time. No, do not touch him! As of this moment Sir Malacaster Kark is in the hands of my friend and colleague Doctor Watson."

"I think not," rasped another voice, behind us. "Sir Malacaster is my patient and any intervention by Doctor Watson would be quite unethical. Stand back, I say!"

"By all means," retorted Holmes, suavely, reaching above the bed and turning up the gas, "but first let us throw some light on our surroundings."

The sudden incandescence revealed the newcomer to be a man of middle height and years, with nothing to distinguish him other than a pronounced limp, the extent of which was apparent when he moved closer. "I will thank you to keep your meddlesome ways to yourself," he barked, leaning on his cane. "I am the master of this establishment."

"With an agreeable bedside manner," mocked Holmes. "You are as courteous to visitors as you are considerate of your patient's welfare."

"He cannot see or hear us", shrugged the other.

"Small wonder! He is in a drugged stupor!"

"I do not intend to bandy words with a common house-breaker!"

"Nor I with a rogue and a murderer, Doctor Marriot Jaymes!"

"Are you mad?"

"Mad enough to know that your victim did not die of apoplexy!"

"Suppose I humour you in your delusion, Mr Sherlock Holmes - from what other cause do you claim Mr Treasure Fortune died?"

"I see that you know who I am. Just as I know that death was effected by means of a pellet of cyanide of the same size and colour as a pearl of caviar."

"Which was fired into his mouth from an air-pistol!"

"Nothing so direct, but I grant the idea is quite as ingenious as that employed ... which was to drop the pellet on to the plate while attention was fixed on your hired agitator in a sandwich-board.

"Dropped? Dropped, did you say?" The crippled doctor laughed scornfully. "By some passing bird? Your imagination knows no bounds, Mr Holmes."

"While the evil of yours found expression in the use of a Borgia ring, so fashioned that it might be sprung open and its deadly cargo released without fear of detection. Remark the circumstances: a pointing finger ... a moment of contrived distraction ... the ring so that its poison-cupboard points downward ... and Hey Presto! the seed is sown. The one flaw in an otherwise perfect plan was imposed by the seating arrangements, which meant that the ring was worn on the index finger of the right hand. And which finger," Holmes wound up triumphantly, indicating the sick man's exposed hands, "is bare of any ornamentation!"

"That is as may be," interposed Mr Armitage Lamb, speaking for the first time since we had entered the room, "but I will not tolerate this vicious slander of a good and honourable man."

"I assure you that the villain of the piece is neither the one nor the other."

"I am referring to Sir Malacaster Kark."

"Whose honour is not impugned."

"It is so by Implication, by Inference and by Innuendo. You forget, Sir, that I am a solicitor first and a town clerk second, and I warn you that if you persist in this monstrous defamation you may live to regret it."

"Dear me," commented Holmes, with a smile, "you are a lamb by name and a lion by nature! This being so, your hunting instinct will lead you to conclude that Sir Malacaster was in an unique position to carry out the actions I have described."

"Then you do indict him?"

"He is in no position to indict anyone," put in Doctor Jaymes, contemptuously. "You forget that Mr Treasure

25

Fortune is alive and well!"

"Quite true," admitted Sherlock Holmes, but it does not mean that an individual bearing that name was not fatally poisoned."

"Oh come, Mr Holmes," protested Armitage Lamb, "what kind of a riddle is this?"

"Not a riddle, but a most accomplished personation. Ah, I thought that would startle you. It was an almost faultless performance by an unknown but gifted thespian recruited by Mr Treasure Fortune in order that he himself might appear to be where he was not. Though an ambitious man, he is also an exceedingly lazy one, who sought to avoid the task of electioneering while seeming assiduously to undertake it."

Throughout this most lucid yet astonishing explanation, my mind had become host to a chaos of thoughts and emotions. That such things had taken place in the peaceful heartland of England was, to me, deeply disturbing, for although I had long ago come to realize that politics is a dirty business I had never expected to see its escutcheon so sullied by death and deceit. It was, I think, the deception that affected me so deeply, not only because it was the cloak employed by a pusillanimous politician, but because the same unsavoury garment had been used to deny the very existence of a fellow human being. It was as if all that I valued and believed in had been torn to pieces, and in a sudden blaze of indignation I rounded upon Mr Sherlock Holmes and told him so.

"There is justice in what you say, Watson," he conceded, "and I am of the opinion that the Government has blundered badly in its handling of the situation. It is ironical, to say the least, when the instigator of a crime is enjoined officially to contradict it, while a sergeant of police is prevented from upholding the law."

"But why was it necessary to go to these lengths? One would think that England is at the mercy of a gang of cutthroats."

"To avoid a scandal. And the possible dissolution of Parliament. As to the country, you are closer to the truth than you realize."

"Good Lord, Holmes, you don't say so! But look here, I can appreciate poor Cobb's predicament, but if what you say of Doctor Jaymes is true why should he co-operate with our people in hushing matters up?"

"Self preservation, my dear fellow. Having come to the notice of the powers that be, it was in his own interests to keep quiet. At some future date he would doubtless select another target and strike again, for it is congruent with his aims to create in England a state of anarchy."

"The fact remains," insisted Mr Armitage Lamb, "that a man has been murdered, and that the finger of suspicion points at my friend Sir Malacaster Kark."

"And would demonstrate his guilt, were it not for the fact that he was not in the Town Hall at the material time."

"Nonsense! I sat next to him!"

"And chatted about this and that?"

"Certainly."

"Yet we have it on the testimony of Sergeant Kirby that Sir Malacaster and Mr Treasure Fortune discussed only their schooldays."

"What is strange in that?"

"The strangeness lies in the fact that they agreed so readily, when it would have been natural, occasionally, to do otherwise."

"Which suggests?"

"That what each had learned by rote he dare not modify, for not only was one man an imposter..."

"By Jove, Holmes!" I exclaimed, "you do not mean..."

"That is exactly what I mean, Watson. The Sir Malacaster Kark of the evening was a substitute also."

"And where is he now?"

"Listening at the door, I fancy. No, no, Watson, let him go. It is after ten o'clock and the police are at the gate.

"You fiend!" Doctor Marriot Jaymes swung his cane with all the force at his command. "You have read every twist and turn of my mind."

"And anticipated this assault," drawled Holmes, coolly parrying the blow. "Watson, please be so good as to cover this criminal lunatic with your revolver."

When the situation was thus under control, I ventured to ask Holmes how it was that with the real Sir Malacaster imprisoned in his sick-bed his gaoler had risked much by allowing Mr Armitage Lamb to pay him a visit.

"But don't you see, Watson?" cried Sherlock Holmes, his eyes flashing, "It is the most heartless element in the entire plot, for if Sir Malacaster can be seen to be in serious decline, his eventual demise will come as no surprise."

"But why should it be necessary to do away with him, if that is what you are implying?"

"Really, Watson, I should have thought the answer is obvious. He cannot be kept in a drugged condition for ever, and should he be allowed to recover who knows what story he may tell?

"As for his would-be assassin, I have already stated that the evil ambition of Doctor Marriot Jaymes is the ruin of this great nation of ours. That he has so far failed is due in no small measure to the integrity of a provincial policeman, and to the unique qualities of an ex-sergeant of marines*."

"And the Right Honourable Treasure Fortune will continue in office, I presume?"

"For the time being, yes. But then, if I am not mistaken, he will be forced into the obscurity he so richly deserves. And now, Watson, if you will keep a firm grip on your revolver, we will introduce our friend to the constabulary."

"And prefer charges, I dare say?" sneered Jaymes. "In which event I may yet gain my ends. The outcome will rock the Establishment!

* Holmes is here guilty of a solecism: men who have served in the Royal Marines are referred to as former, not as ex.

"Your stay with the police will be short," replied Holmes sternly, as we marched our man out. "I have it on the authority of one who in matters of this sort not merely acts on behalf of the British Government but is the British Government that, should things fall out as I anticipated, you and your accomplice will be handed over to the Secret Service."

"But, Holmes!"

"Watson, these are deep waters, in which lurk renegades and murderers who have by their actions forfeited all normal rights. I am satisfied that the Secret Service is the appropriate instrument of State to invoke."

But in so saying Mr Sherlock Holmes was to be guilty of an uncharacteristic error of judgement, for there occurred upon our return to London a most singular sequel to our cause.

I had visited the Diogenes Club, in Pall Mall, on one previous occasion, when I accompanied Holmes to consult with his brother Mycroft in the perplexing matter of the Greek Interpreter (8), and I was, therefore, prepared for the total silence that was imposed upon us until we were closeted with the portly Mycroft in the Strangers' Room.

He was as I remembered him - sharp of expression, yet having a far-away introspective look in his watery-grey eyes.

"This is the very devil of a game, Sherlock," he began, when we were seated. "Quite the worst in my experience."

"I am in complete agreement," replied Holmes. "That is why I took the extreme step of contacting you by means of the telephone. I trust that you were not unpardonably inconvenienced?"

"Not at all." The massive head moved fractionally from side to side. "That is not the reason I wished to see you. As you know, it was my intention that Marriot Jaymes and his creature should be disposed of by the Secret Service."

Mycroft held out a slip of paper. And when his brother looked up from a scrutiny of it: "It had escaped you, then?"

"Yes," responded Sherlock, with a queer thrill in his voice. "It had escaped me."

"And now he has escaped us!"

"What!"

"The lame foot was a sham. He was out of the carriage door while the train bringing him here was going at forty miles-an-hour. The police and the waterguard are on watch, of course, but so far he has eluded them."

"And will continue to do so," predicted Sherlock Holmes, bitterly "A state of affairs for which I hold myself entirely responsible."

"Do not reproach yourself, Sherlock. Even I did not make the connection until it was too late. That he is a master of disguise is one thing, that he should create for himself a new identity in a remote part of the country is undeniably brilliant. The man is a criminal virtuoso, with the brain of a genius and the body of a chameleon."

For a time there was complete silence in the room, with only the street scenes beyond the bow-window to remind one that life went on. "I may be a dullard," I ventured, acutely aware that I was in the company of not one master of logic but of two, "but am I to understand that the doctor has escaped?"

"Doctor my foot!" snarled Sherlock Holmes, tossing over the slip of paper. "See for yourself! The name Marriot Jaymes is an anagram, the letters of which also spell James Moriarty!" (9)

Footnotes

1. As indicated in Watson's introduction, the name is fictitious in order to protect the identity of the person concerned. This is no doubt also true of other personalities central to the narrative

2. The train Holmes evidently had in mind was that from Euston to Manchester London Road (as it then was), which departed at noon (and not at five minutes past, as he supposed) and was due at its destination at 4.20 pm. It is probable that Holmes and Watson then crossed Manchester to the Lancashire & Yorkshire Railway's Victoria Station, or to the Exchange Station next to it. They could, for example, have taken the 5.45

A photograph from the Moriarty family album, lent to Dr Watson
by Mrs Shelagh Vincent (see page 118). Said to be the infant
James Moriarty carrying a toy (?) gun.

pm Midland train from Victoria and been in Blackburn at 6.34 pm. But the actual destination is open to conjecture.

3. Parliamentary trains were formerly those carrying passengers at a rate of not more than one penny a mile, and which every railway company was obliged by Act of Parliament to run daily each way over its system. Holmes is here no doubt employing the term in the sense of a slow, stopping train, which, according to the time-table in Note 2 he and Watson almost certainly had to endure on the second leg of their journey.

4. Holmes is here drawing attention to the fact that cyanide of potassium is characterized by the intense smell of bitter almonds. Found in nature in bitter almonds and in peach and apricot pits, cyanide is a swift-acting poison, with the ability to bind the body's breathing mechanism.

5. Steam trams were used extensively in parts of Lancashire at this time, not least because many routes were too steep for horses. In Burnley, for example, the 'steamers' were introduced in the town in 1881, and were kept in service until the advent of the first electric cars in 1901.

6. Watson's choice of the word 'ringing' is particularly apt, for it was a then characteristic of northern industrial towns that there was about them a distinctive echoing or 'ringing' quality of sound, especially at night, brought about by the admixture of cold, carrying breezes, streets paved with cobbles (or sets), and the clog-irons worn by the working classes.

7. One so constructed that, although the light burned continuously, the illumination could be cut off by means of a shutter. It was a feature of most dark lanterns that the shutter acted as a reflector when positioned behind the flame, which was itself located behind a convex lens.

8. First published in The *Strand* Magazine, in 1893. Mycroft Holmes, who featured prominently in the story, had lodgings in Pall Mall, opposite the Diogenes Club, of which he was a founder member.

9. It would appear that if, as seems chronologically to be the case, Professor James Moriarty assumed the identity of Doctor Marriot Jaymes subsequent to 4th May, 1891, he not only survived his splash into the Reichenbach Falls, but was thereafter twice the man!

Coffins at Candlemas
A Riddle of the Ribble Valley

Of the manifold experiences I shared with Mr Sherlock
Holmes, one of the most singular is that which unfolded
during the early part of the year 1895, when we were caught
up in events so bizarre that they remain fixed in my mind as
is a fly in amber.

No less vividly do I recall the sub-arctic severity of that
memorable winter (¹). It had snowed on and off for several
weeks; then from the nones of January to the ides of that
month it snowed without pause. And while the thick white
carpet was yet new, its pile upstanding, there came from the
Steppes of Russia, and thence by way of Finland and the
Gulf of Bothnia, a wind that crisped the snow and sealed
with icy hands every drop of exposed water.

The supine surfaces of the ponds and lakes submitted
first, looking by day like frosted glass and by night like
mirrors misted by the breath of the moon. The canals
capitulated also, the water in the locks seemingly taken in
mid stride. Next the rivers, great and small, their final
struggles marked, where the flow ran swiftest, by the frozen
fury of their thwarted passage; and at their meetings, by the
crystallized permanence of their embrace. Even the margins
of the seas succumbed.

So intense was the cold, and so abiding, that in the space
of a week its puissance had locked the land in elemental
gyves and fetters, prompting the fanciful to whisper about
the coming of another ice-age. But as the populace at large
adapted to the glacial conditions and went about their
business, so the snow became compacted and not
inconducive to travel. Horse-drawn conveyances still plied
the highways and byways, and some enterprising souls fitted
skies in the place of wheels, while on the rink-like surface of

the Thames there was skating and tobogganing and foolhardy pilgrimages from one bank to the other.

Had this exceptional weather not persisted, the happenings I am about to relate would not have been possible. And had the hansom I was riding in on a particular morning late in January not skidded on the polished camber of Baker Street and broken a shaft, I should not have found myself marooned without the door of number 221B and so become involved in these happenings.

I had not lodged there since just before the turn of the year, when at the request of young Verner ([2]) I had returned as *locum tenens* to my old practice in Kensington, and to find Holmes huddled in the basket chair, looking shabby and unkempt, came as a considerable shock. His black hair, normally swept back from his high forehead, hung long and lank, and a dun-coloured dressing-gown, carelessly tied, gaped above his updrawn knees, while the petulant sucking at an oily pipe, as well as creating an evil-smelling fug, served to register the pallor of his unbarbered cheeks.

It was apparent that he was in the grip of an almost catatonic ennui, which malady all too often overtook him when a prolonged period of boredom aggravated the depressive side of his mercurial nature. But I looked in vain for the needle, concluding with a profound sense of relief that however low his spirit had plunged he was no yet so far drained of will that he had returned to the habit that had once threatened his health and strained our friendship.

"You have not breakfasted," I scolded him, glancing from the unlaid table to the nascent flames of an infant fire. "The bottom has dropped out of the glass, and you are without warmth from food or fossil."

"They mean nothing to me."

"I would that you were as dismissive of tobacco," I retorted as yet another puff of greasy smoke coiled upwards. "It may interest you to know, " I added, throwing off my hat and coat and sitting unbidden in the chair facing his, "that some tests I have conducted indicate that the presence of nicotine in the system so constricts the arterial vessels that the blood pressure is raised."

"My, my, Watson, you have become quite the specialist since taking up your new post, not to say a busy and handsomely retained one: the inky indentation towards the tip of the middle finger of your right hand suggests an abundance of note making and prescription writing. Off hand I would say that in the few months he has been there Verner has at least doubled your old panel."

"The terms `busy' and `handsomely retained' are not mutually inclusive, Holmes."

He waved a limp hand. "Oh, there are several pointers as to the latter. The label stitched into your new Chesterfield is Eli Grossman's, who cuts for the Prince of Wales. Then there is the interesting little matter of your top hat."

"But I am not wearing a top hat."

"That is the little matter I find interesting. Your preference for a Homburg draws attention to the fact that, being unable to accommodate a stethoscope between your two crowns, you no doubt do so in the also new Gladstone resting between your feet. The bag is an expensive one, Watson, and is in its way every bit as illuminating as the gold leaf used to personalize it."

"Really, Holmes!" I protested. "My owning a decent overcoat and a better-than-average bag stamped with my initials is scant evidence that I am flush as well as busy."

"It is when the boots on your feet show by their fit that each has its own last."

That he had accurately deduced that I had splashed out on bespoke pair of balmorals was really quite astonishing. "Your powers are as acute as ever," I assured him.

"Pooh! I am like a trained dog. My senses convey the data to my brain, which produces a conditioned response.

"Nonsense! You see it thus because you are in the doldrums just now. I'll wager that upon encountering some new and vital challenge, you will be as completely in command of your responses as I am certain such a challenge will shortly present itself."

No sooner had I cast this double-barrelled hostage to fortune, than my gloomy companion remarked that there was someone pulling at the door bell.

"Yes, Mrs Hudson, what is it?"

"A Miss Blaze Carrick asking to see you, Mr Holmes."

"Of Pendleroyd Hall," supplied our young and eager visitor, when the housekeeper had departed, "near the town of Clitheroe, in the County of Lancaster."

Withdrawing one slim hand from within her muff, she drew back the hood of her plain brown travelling cloak and took a small, determined step closer. "I am come," she continued, shaking aside the cluster of auburn curls which contrived to hide the arresting greenness of her wide-set eyes, "to consult Mr Sherlock Holmes concerning the disappearance of my dear father, Sir Giles Carrick."

"I recommend that you address your complaint to the official police," mumbled Holmes, not troubling to rise, "who are not without experience in such matters."

"The police are baffled, Mr Holmes."

"Oh, very well, Miss Blaze Carrick of Pendleroyd, do you sit here, in the ladderback and you shall have five minutes to state why I should seek your father."

"I may state it in five seconds, Mr Holmes. I believe he has been foully murdered."

For the space of time it took a passing omnibus to rattle our windows, she held his gaze, the pale oval of her face washed pink by the light from the now brightly burning fire.

"Data, my dear young lady, I must have data," sighed Sherlock Holmes. "Without it I can do nothing, formulate no hypothesis."

"If you mean do I have proof, Mr Holmes, I have none save the God-given knowledge that there is evil in the air at Pendleroyd. I feel it, I breath it, I can almost reach out and touch it."

"But can you measure it? Or describe it? Or point to its lair? The Royal Borough of Clitheroe (^{3}) lies on the northern fringe of Pendle witch country (4), does it not? Possibly it is that old evil you perceive?"

"The shades of Demdike and Chattox and those other poor wretches taken as witches (5) nearly three hundred years ago have not hitherto troubled me."

"*Touché*," murmured Holmes, with a quirky smile. "Well, Miss Carrick, what I have so far heard persuades me to hear more. If an hour will suffice, my time is yours. What about you, Watson?"

"My rounds this morning are more social than medical."

Thus encouraged, Miss Carrick released the clasp of her cloak and what remained of a long-held breath. "It all began in the late summer of last year," she explained, "when my Uncle Rufus descended upon us. I knew then that someone special had entered our lives, for the man who stood arm-in-arm with my father had about him an air of power and purpose. He was as tall and tanned and as lean and fair as I had imagined - that being my notion of a naval officer - but younger looking and less formal.

"'My brother has invited me, now that I am done with the Royal Navy, to make my home at Pendleroyd,' my uncle greeted me. 'I shall trade heavily on the patience of you both in finding my place here.'

"It was well said, Mr Holmes, and as we sat at dinner that same evening I confess that I weighed the two men: my father who by virtue of progenitor had inherited Pendleroyd Hall and all that went with it, and the recent post captain, who as a boy of fifteen had gone to sea as a midshipman and had endured the iron discipline of the greatest navy in the world. My uncle sparkled where his brother lacked lustre, and seeing them thus - the one bright and quick of wit, the other dull and slow - told how joyless were our lives at Pendleroyd Hall."

"But it was not always so?" probed Holmes.

"Only since the hunt claimed the life of my mother, four summers ago."

"A sadness which recent events promise to assuage," murmured Sherlock Holmes. "Tell, me, Miss Carrick," he continued, in a businesslike way, "were you privy to your uncle's impending arrival?" And when she said that she was not: "And did he say on what account he had left Her Majesty's Service?"

"Only that with the Dogs of War in Europe safely kennelled the Admiralty has scant use for the likes of him."

"He is a bachelor, I take it?"

"He is - or was - married only to the sea, Mr Holmes."

"And he is the younger of the two brothers. Is he perhaps also your father's only brother?"

"As I am my father's only child."

"And how old a child is that, Miss Carrick?"

"I shall shortly be three-and-twenty," she owned.

During these exchanges Mr Sherlock Holmes had by degrees reverted more nearly to the man I admired and respected. As well as emerging from the attack of *taedium vitae* and becoming alert in manner and incisive of speech, he had pushed from his brow the dark hank of hair and thrown into the hearth his burned-out clay.

"You were lamenting Pendleroyd's lost social pleasures," he prompted, harking back.

"For which I sought compensation in the company of my uncle," she readily admitted. "In the days and weeks that followed his coming we were much together. There were places of local interest to revisit: the Norman castle overlooking the approaches to Clitheroe, and a few miles to the west, at Whalley, what remained of de Lacy's Cistercian abbey. There were shopping expeditions to towns as distant as Blackburn and Preston; and there was the demesne to be ridden, when my uncle met with a cordiality touching upon hope, as if his presence might herald a return to the time when the Hall was the hub of affairs in this part of the Ribble Valley, and the Carricks were looked to for leadership and a sense of duty."

"*Noblesse oblige*," murmured Holmes. Then, in his most judicial tone: "If your father has in some way forfeited the community's trust and respect, I must insist upon knowing the cause and extent of the disaffection."

"You ask too much, Mr Holmes."

"I dare not ask less, Miss Carrick."

"Then I must decline to answer."

"As I must decline to continue this consultation. If you will kindly ring the bell, Watson, Mrs Hudson shall show the young lady out."

I was not anxious to do Holmes's bidding, and it pleased me when Miss Carrick capitulated, if with a touch of ginger, "Very well, Mr Sherlock Holmes, you shall know the truth, the whole truth, and nothing but the truth, on the condition that what is divulged shall not without my consent pass beyond these walls."

"You have my solemn word," said he.

"And mine," said I.

"What I have earlier confided concerning my father's condition," Miss Carrick resumed, after taking a moment to compose herself, "is but the tip of the iceberg. Not only was he solitary of habit and withdrawn in mind since my mother's death, but fumbling and unreliable from too much wine. When in his cups and melancholy with it, I feared for his reason, dreadful of the day when he should be removed to the asylum or confined in some secret room at Pendleroyd Hall."

"And what path did his affliction take when he suffered most?"

"A dangerous one, Mr Holmes. At such times he took to wandering abroad, often in the dead of night."

"And what transpired?"

The madness passed, and he had no memory of it." She blinked away a tear. "But the intervals grew shorter."

"And his tenants impatient, even angry," nodded Holmes. "You have described the situation admirably, Miss Carrick. Kindly continue your most interesting narrative."

Again she sought to compose herself, twisting and pulling at the muff in her lap. "Changes," she said eventually, "were thus seen to be desirable as well as desired, and as my uncle shouldered the affairs of the demesne, so my father willingly surrendered them. And so matters stood at the turn of the year, when Rufus - he had used my Christian name from the first, Mr Holmes, and lately had urged me to use his - when Rufus and I rode the few miles to Hodderholm Manor.

"Simon and Lydia Farthingale are old and dear friends of the family, and although Lydia is twenty years my senior she has always treated me as a sister, and I found it strange that she now appeared stiff and somewhat guarded."

"Towards whom?"

"Towards Rufus. It was as if she sought to keep him at arms' length, as one would a social climber, or an interloper. But he is none of these, Mr Holmes," she added, with a defiant tilt of her chin. "He is my father's brother, and a fine and honourable man."

"How did Mr Simon Farthingale comport himself?"

"Loudly," she smiled. "Simon mixes the rôle of businessman with that of country squire, and announced that in order to spend more time in Lancaster he had appointed a gentleman steward to manage the estate. It was when Rufus asked if we might meet him that Lydia most exampled the stiffness I have spoken of, declaring Mr John Storm to be averse to any form of social intercourse."

Holmes shrugged the disclosure aside. "I am not myself of a gregarious nature."

"Nevertheless, the incident jarred, Mr Holmes, and was soon joined by another, though not this time of Lydia Farthingale's making. We had returned almost to Pendleroyd Hall, when we were overtaken by a trap transporting a solitary passenger. As the trap drew ahead and then stopped at the house, its black-garbed occupant appeared to alight without first rising, like a sun-stunned beetle falling from a sill. Coming close, I perceived that the beetle was female: a squat, strongly-built woman of middle age wearing a poke bonnet and a waisted coat buttoned over a bombazine frock, the braided hem of which scuffed the pointed toes of cracked walking boots."

"Were you frightened of this woman?" I interposed. "Or in some way intimidated by her?"

"Not then, Doctor Watson. Curious, yes. And I confess that when I stared into the dark tunnel of her bonnet and saw a band of coarse dark hair drawn across a broad forehead, and cheeks pouched like dry leather on either side of a fleshy nose, I suffered the remarkable sensation of having my own cheeks turn crimson with vexation while my body strove to repress a shudder of revulsion.

"I remember thinking how impassive she looked, like the beetle I had first taken her for. And how much lighter the trap when her luggage - a brass-bound, hump-lidded trunk with the initials `AG' burned into the oak - followed her to the ground.

"Imagine my astonishment when Rufus turned to me and said: `This is Mrs Alice George, our new housekeeper, come to ease the burden of your domestic duties. She hails from Manchester, and has just now arrived off the Blackburn connection'."

"The time?" cried Sherlock Holmes. "What time of the day did this encounter take place?"

"It was a little after noon, Mr Holmes. The factory hooter at Chatburn (6) had just sounded."

"Well, well," he approved, rubbing his sinewy hands together, "there is no gainsaying a factory hooter. Make a long arm, Watson, there's a good fellow, and reach down the *Bradshaw*. Ha! Hum! Yes, I thought so." And after riffling the pages again: "Capital! There is an express out of Euston for Preston at ten. You shall continue your narrative *en train*, Miss Carrick."

"But..."

"But me no buts. Time is of the essence, my dear young lady." For desperate seconds she stared out of the window, as if afraid of returning to the frozen world without. Then, snatching those remarkable eyes away from the mirthless grin of the icicles depending from the eves, she said simply: "If I might first call at my hotel in Wigmore Street, I am in your hands, Mr Holmes."

"Excellent! And what of you, Watson? Do you leave a note for young Verner's return tomorrow, I shall be delighted to have you along."

"Certainly, Holmes," I responded. "But how the devil did you apprehend Verner's return?"

"When the *locum tenens* declares his rounds this morning social rather than medical, it is a sure sign he is expecting the arrival of the regular man. But do come along, both of you! The Palatine express departs in barely thirty minutes (7) ..."

***

Given the conditions, our journey north was understandably slow, and we were shortly glad of the small hamper Mrs Hudson had thrust upon us. Glad, too, of the diversion promised by the continuation of Miss Blaze Carrick's account of events in a place yet some two hundred miles distant. That she was a most resilient individual was exemplified by her willingness at such peremptory notice to return there, pausing only at the station telegraph to wire her intention ahead.

"We had just now been introduced to the unprepossessing Mrs Alice George," prompted Holmes, swaddling more deeply into his Inverness.

"And I to a nightmare," shuddered Miss Carrick. "In my dreams that night there was a black shape bearing down on me ... now in the form of a great fat beetle ... now as a looming storm-cloud, like those which in summer come upon us from the west and linger at the confluence of the Calder and the Ribble before taking one water-path or the other. Next in my dream there was a sound like thunder, and a bright light spinning like St Elmo's fire at the ragged inter-face of earth and sky ... then there came another clap ... and I sat up in bed to find that the thunder had been the sound of shutters being opened by my maid, and that the lightning was a flashing curtain of white beyond the window-glass ..."

The imagery was compelling, and Holmes and I waited in hushed expectation of its predicate.

"It snowed," Miss Carrick resumed eventually, "for the span the old wives divined, and when it ceased with a last wild flurry, as if the Great Hill of Pendle (8) had like a shaggy dog risen from the hearth of the cotton towns (9) and shaken itself, the demesne was seen to slumber beneath a mantle that dazzled by day and shone by night."

"And within?" pressed Holmes, in that shrewd, intuitive way he has.

"Within, it seemed that every door at Pendleroyd Hall opened upon the black-garbed figure of Mrs George. Even Rufus stood in awe of her, excusing her surliness as reserve, her intrusions as anxiety to give satisfaction."

"And Sir Giles, your father?"

"Perceived none of this. Lately he petitioned the bottle constantly, his faculties as clouded as the dregs he tippled. Do you wonder?" she asked, leaning forward in her seat and fixing Sherlock Holmes with a gaze that matched the intensity of his, "that as soon as conditions allowed I took to riding out alone?" She sank back against the cushion. "Only to return one day to news so frightful that I did not at first fully comprehend it."

The express was steaming hard now, the white flanks of the Midland Plain escaping in a blur the ice-starred windows of our compartment. Shortly, with a percussion which assaulted our ears, we raced into a tunnel, and when with equal suddenness we emerged Miss Carrick opened her tight-shut eyes and said: "After I set out that afternoon, it seems my father determined to visit the home farm. Rufus tried to dissuade him, but Father insisted."

"How was Sir Giles in himself?"

"I suspect that his wits sat as heavy in his head as his boots in the stirrups. The best that could be done was to saddle up his quietest horse, and this Rufus ensured."

"But no one accompanied your father?"

"He forbad it."

"Or followed?"

"Rufus did as soon as his own horse was ready."

"Taking the same route?"

"Taking the only route, Mr Holmes. Then and now the lane to home farm lies between banks of hard-packed snow. And yet when Rufus found Strickland, the farm manager, neither had seen anything of my father."

"Where, exactly, was Strickland?"

"In the mill loft, mending a broken paddle."

"And Mrs Strickland and those others who are employed there?"

"Avoiding Mrs George, no doubt. None of them can bear her poking and prying."

"Mrs George, you say? What was her business at home farm?"

"When the big freeze came there was a generally expressed wish for a *fête champêtre*, and Father gave permission for it to be held at home farm. Mrs George assumed charge of the arrangements, and undertook to root out anything which might serve."

"What of your father's horse?" asked Holmes, changing tack.

"Ned came in the next morning, wet to his knees and hocks but otherwise unmarked."

"That is most interesting," commented Sherlock Holmes when the train wheels had ceased their rumble over a girder bridge, "but please be so good as to continue from the time Sir Giles was judged lost."

"When Rufus returned to the Hall empty handed it was already dark, and soon afterwards the Superintendent of police at Clitheroe caused his constables to ask after my father wherever their beats took them. He also mustered a small army of volunteers - shepherds, villagers, demesne workers and the like - to assist his men in making a systematic search of the area."

"And this that first night?"

"And deep into the night. And again at dawn. And that day and night also."

As Sir Giles Carrick's brave and deeply wounded daughter spoke out, the catch in her voice and the heave of her bosom eloquent of her distress, I knew beyond peradventure that she had as well searched her own heart and soul lest some thoughtless word or deed of hers had lent wings to her father's going. Just as I knew that each passing hour had returned smaller hope of his being found alive. Or of his being found at all, for the prevailing conditions, if rendering the search arduous, enabled the police to eliminate as a place of concealment every inch of open water; all such

45

places - not least the lake at home farm - being visited and their carapaces found innocent of breach.

"So what remains?" I ventured.

"What remains, Doctor Watson, is that my father was either thrown by his horse into a drift, and the place obscured by the comings and goings of others, or he has, as I believe, met with foul play and his body in some way disposed of."

"But not the victim of witchcraft?" hazarded Holmes.

"Even that has been whispered. It seems that the date set for the winter fair marks both Candlemas (10) and a witches' sabbat (11)."

"The second day of February," said I, shocked into recollection. "Just two days hence. What devilry awaits us between now and then, Holmes?"

"We must prepare for the very worst, Watson. It is my belief that the stews of London's Whitechapel do not conceal viler sin than does the bland face of the English countryside, and when that face is glazed and powdered by Nature the opportunities for evil are infinitely greater.

And infinitely more difficult of detection. The corollary needed no spoken words of mine to clothe it, and as the express began its run through the scatter of buildings that heralded our approach to the considerable northern town of Preston, I was constrained to think of the writings of Mr Edgar Allan Poe, and of his account of the murders in the Rue Morgue. That crime took place in an apparently locked room, whereas Sir Giles Carrick had vanished from a demonstrably locked world, and I fell to wondering if even the unique deductive powers of Mr Sherlock Holmes could succeed in unravelling a mystery which the official police, with their superior resources and intimate knowledge of the locality, had so far found impenetrable.

Thought of the police prompted me to inquire of Miss Carrick the name of the official who had charge of the case.

"An Inspector Strap," she replied, "of the Lancaster Detective Department."

"Oh, that will be Inspector Indigo Strap (12)," commented Holmes, "whom I was pleased to give a pointer or two when Chief Constable Bullivant sought my help over the Lune salmon scandal a few years ago. Strap is an able enough fellow, if sometimes acting the buffoon. But here we are at Preston Fishergate," he added, rising and consulting the watch he drew from its fob, "precisely one hour and ten minutes behind schedule."

**

To record that the remainder of our journey was one of body- and mind-numbing tedium is to understate the case, not least on account of its taking almost as long to travel some forty miles sideways as the express had taken to steam from London. Stops and starts were frequent, with much lurching and jolting, not only at obscure country halts but for no apparent reason. That my two travelling companions appeared indifferent to these vicissitudes - Holmes ensconced Sphinx-like in his corner seat, and Miss Carrick, now regarding the darkling scene beyond the compartment windows, now reclining composed and stoically uncomplaining in hers - served only to aggravate my longings for a hot meal and a comfortable bed; which state of mind persisted until, at last, we reached Clitheroe.

There were no other passengers to alight, and my most abiding recollections are of a townscape upon which the chill blackness of the night pressed with proprietorial weight against the contrasting whiteness that thatched each and every house and building, and of a station yard devoid of any means of onward transportation save a solitary conveyance so still and dark that for one startled moment I took it for a hearse, but which proved to be a brougham sent to await our arrival.

Clitheroe Station

Having carried Holmes and me only as far as the summit of King Street and thus hard by the doors of the Swan and Royal Hotel, the brougham bore Miss Blaze Carrick away, its lamps casting pools of yellow light on the rutted surface of the highway. That it should in the morning return in order to convey us to Pendleroyd Hall seemed a relatively distant prospect, but the cheerful atmosphere of the posting inn, the enjoyment of good food, a slow-burning Havana, and a tolerable claret, consummated by eight hours in a feather bed lent wings to the clock, and all too soon Holmes and I were again up and about, breakfasted on eggs and rashers, and once more passengers in the promised brougham.

Soon the Royal Borough of Clitheroe was behind us, its Norman Castle (13) framed in the small window at our backs, while alongside, to our left, reposed the northern flank of the Great Hill of Pendle, the vast, rounded bulk reminiscent of a beached white whale. But now we were edging into a tunnel-like byway, banked snow scraping the sides of the brougham, eventually to debouch into the village of Pendleton, keeping company for a time with a deep-sided iced-over stream.

Perhaps half a mile on, breaking to the left, the horses turned in through the open gates of Pendleroyd Hall, a squat, stone-built mansion house set like a sturdy footstool at the western extremity of Pendle Hill. Shortly, we drew up at the portals of the Hall, whence we were conducted without ceremony into an oak-panelled ante-chamber and thence into a sombre morning-room barely warmed by a smoky fire and as poorly illuminated by the watery light of the sun slanting through narrow mullioned windows.

Besides Miss Blaze Carrick, who welcomed us with an urgent smile, two others awaited our entry, one a tall, straight-backed man whose plain garb did nothing to dispel the impression of the recent naval officer, the other, a stocky, long-nosed individual conspicuous in a buttoned-up snuff-coloured coat and matching knickerbockers, who clutched to his chest the open side of a curly-brimmed brown bowler hat. Such were our introductions to Captain Rufus Carrick and Inspector Indigo Strap.

"You are well come," the former cordially greeted us, using the old form of words. "It is my niece's initiative that brings you here, and you shall be afforded whatever assistance you may require in your endeavours on our behalf."

It was well said, if somewhat spoiled by Strap's booming, "So you shall, Mr Sherlock Holmes; and you likewise, Doctor Wilson."

Rather to my annoyance I observed Holmes suppressing an amused smile. If this country inspector was as eccentric in his methods as in his modes of dress and address, I entertained small hope of his being of service. Yet there was a certain quick brightness about the fellow's gaze that projected an underlying shrewdness of mind, and recalling Holmes's opinion of him I determined to suspend judgement.

Aware perhaps of my somewhat minatory stare, the object of it edged sideways, as if seeking refuge behind a ladder-back chair furnished with an antimacassar. "As I was saying, Miss," Strap resumed, no doubt continuing some earlier discourse, "there is talk, seeing as Sir Giles has vanished into thin air, so to speak ... there is talk that your father might be the victim of witchcraft. "

"Oh, come now, Strap," Rufus Carrick's tone conveyed his contempt. "since when does an inspector of police give credence to old wives' tales?"

"Begging your pardon, Capting," returned Strap, hugging his bowler, "but when does an inspector of police dare to ignore inklings of any complexion, not knowing where they might lead?"

"Just so," murmured Sherlock Holmes. "Indeed, I must hear more of these Pendle witches. Perhaps you, Miss

50

Carrick, will add to what little you have previously told me, so that I might learn how their long shadows impinge on the matter before us."

Her colour rising nearly to match the glow of the red-gold kirtle and sleeved bodice she wore, the girl's curtness when she spoke told of an impatience akin to that of her uncle's. "No doubt Inspector Strap has been listening to my maid, Grace Dempster," declared Blaze, "who stuffs her head with such nonsense."

"And what sort of nonsense would that be?" prompted Holmes.

"That they robbed graves, that they could fly, that they had familiars and conversed with the Devil, that they could bring harm to man and beast, even unto death."

"And what became of them, these Pendle witches?"

"They were hanged, Mr Holmes (14). As to the harm they did, the substance of that reposed more in the minds of the ignorant than within the power of a handful of vindictive old beggar-women. But all this was over three hundred years ago (15); what manner of bearing may it have on the present, other than to foster a miasma of superstition?"

"Which is the very nub of my interest," commented Holmes, in that incisive way of his when he has isolated some point of particular significance. "For there are those, are there not, who feed off such superstition, and who meddle in the Black Arts?"

"Oh, there are such," agreed Blaze. "Grace Dempster's mother - also called Grace - for one, who has a reputation in the Valley for having the second sight and the ability to tell fortunes. Or, as Parson Tobias Catlow has it, of miming to the words of the Devil."

"My niece tells me the old woman augments her wages skivvying for Doctor Braithwaite by reading the tea leaves and by purveying the product of her still-room," Rufus Carrick put in. "And if that is all that she does it is really no business of anyone else, Parson Catlow included. Anything more," he added, fixing Sherlock Holmes with a blue-eyed stare, "is so much mumbo-jumbo. Why, there are some who would lay the coming of this present weather at Old Mother Dempster's door, as they no doubt will its going, should she choose to hint in that direction."

"My, my," smiled Holmes, "potent spells indeed that can cause a fall of snow as well in London as here."

Even so, there was in the air a stirring of elemental images that no amount of rationalization could entirely dispel, and I sensed that my friend, normally the first to reject notions unsupported by fact, was himself aware that here, in these North Parts, where men's minds accommodated myth and legend and ancient shibboleths as readily as reason and logic, it would be a bold, not to say foolish, man who chose to ignore these conflicting aspects of the human condition.

"At all events," opined Inspector Indigo Strap, breaking both by speaking and by drumming his fingers on the crown of his hat the short silence that had overtaken us, "wherever Sir Giles might be he ain't drownded, not with all the water turned to solid ice, he ain't. What say you, Doctor Wilson?"

"Watson," I answered stiffly. "Theoretically, a man could drown in snow were his own body heat sufficient to melt it." It was an unlikely hypothesis, as I well knew, but it at least had the merit of putting the fellow in possession of my correct name and at the same time taking some of the self-important wind out of his sails.

"So what new direction does the mystery take?" demanded Miss Carrick. "Is my father to be looked for indoors, like a mislaid garment? Is that why we are gathered here, when our place is with the search outside?"

"Bless you, no, Miss." Strap's fingers executed another tattoo on his hat. "But the search is only one twig our hopes might perch on." The local man looked appealingly at

Sherlock Holmes, his long face glum between the white celluloid collar and the quiff of sandy hair that lay across a furrowed brow. "Ain't that the truth, Mr Holmes?"

"Just so," conceded Holmes, answering in time to prevent Strap's receiving another scolding from Miss Carrick. "But tell me all that is in train, and pray be precise as to details."

This invitation appealed so much to Indigo Strap that he contrived at one and the same time to dispose of his bowler hat and to produce from a pocket of his jacket an official notebook.

"'The Valley has been scoured from Chatburn to the east as far as Whalley to the west'," he read out. "'And sideways too, particularly at and in the vicinity of home farm'. But the area is vast," he added, looking over the top of his notebook, "and who knows where a gentleman in his condition..."

"Explain yourself," interrupted Rufus Carrick, icily, "lest I find your words offensive."

"How so, Capting?" retorted Strap, snapping shut his notebook. "Because I state a truth and not a slander?'

His directness sent Blaze Carrick's head tossing and her tawny curls swinging. "It seems that gossip finds more ears than flourish in a field of ripe corn."

"And grinds a grain of truth," adjudicated Sherlock Holmes. "Forgive me, Miss Carrick, but Sir Giles's drinking habits could not be as they are and go unremarked, nor fail to be taken into account by the detective department. As I must do," he added.

During these exchanges it occurred to me that thus far we had heard nothing of the *fête champêtre* projected for the celebration of Candlemas, and I ventured to raise the matter.

"I'm sure no one will take it amiss," observed Strap, civilly, addressing Miss Carrick, "should you decide not to go on with it."

"It must go on," she retorted. "If my father was happy in the enterprise, who am I to deny him? Who is anyone?"

These last few words fell like tears in that sombre place, and mixed with the shadows there.

"From whom does any opposition come?" inquired Sherlock Holmes.

"From a single source, and that a potent one. But I shall let the author make his own case, if not by seeking you out, by making the fête his pulpit."

"The fair, then," persisted Holmes, using the English expression. "What form shall it take?"

Here we were on lighter ground, and the girl's manner waxed warm, almost eager. "As I informed you during our journey north, Mr Holmes, the event is to centre on home farm, where the lake that serves the mill is frozen overall to a thickness of many inches."

Sufficient, it seemed, to bear at its edges the stalls and entertainments she enumerated: also, on a cairn, an enormous candle, the making of which was even now proceeding. According to Miss Carrick, the tallow had come from a nearby manufactory, and the wick from the industry of Old Mother Dempster who, skilled in such crafts, had plaited strands of hemp marinaded in lamp oil.

"The candle is to stand within a sheltered contour of the lake," explained Miss Carrick, "as much on the bank as over the water, and will be the focal point of all that ensues."

This much was known, and what she knew Miss Blaze Carrick had divulged openly and without equivocation; yet I formed the opinion that what she knew might be likened to the deceptive appearance of an iceberg, the bulk of which lies beneath the surface, and as Holmes and I took our leave, accompanied by Inspector Indigo Strap, now with his bowler hat squashing the tops of his ears, it came to me that we had left behind us a young woman whose innermost thoughts were not of a candle brightly burning but of a weaker, paler flame that had somehow vanished from the face of the earth.

"Well, well," remarked Sherlock Holmes, as Strap and I

sat facing him in the trap taking us on to home farm, "a pretty little puzzle and no mistake."

During our time at Pendleroyd Hall he had refrained from smoking, but was now drawing with gusto on a pipe I had not seen him use before, a large meerschaum-lined affair with a deeply-curving stem (16). "So what do you make of it all?" he asked, between puffs.

"What am I to make of it, Holmes? A man is vanished, apparently into thin air; the neighbourhood has been turned inside out and upside down, without his being found; his daughter is convinced he has been done away with, yet has not one shred of evidence to that end; all we do know is that the missing man is a toper and is half mad. On top of that," I concluded, with a frowning glance at the slopes of Pendle Hill sweeping up before us, "we are asked to believe that his going might be due to witchcraft. I confess myself baffled."

"Oh, pooh!" chided Holmes, exhaling with evident satisfaction a cloud of grey smoke, "you have omitted to mention the evidence of Sir Giles Carrick's horse."

"But the horse returned in good order."

"That is the evidence to which I refer."

"How so, Mr Holmes?" interjected Strap, directing at me an amused glance. "Am I to understand that I should have taken a statement from the animal?"

"There is also to be looked into the question of the Chatburn factory hooter," continued Holmes, imperturbably.

"But that was earlier," said I.

"Precisely," said he. "But here we are at home farm."

Seen abruptly, as the trap took a bend in the snow-banked lane, the unrelieved stillness of the place embodied a desolate kind of beauty, the hard lines of the mill-house and the sprawl of outbuildings standing forth with the sharpness of lines drawn in charcoal on very white paper.

"Aye, and there's Strickland waiting on us," supplemented Strap.

Strickland was a big man, and strong looking, with a jaw like a spade. It was said of him, I was to learn later, that he rarely smiled and had never been heard to laugh. He was neither laughing nor smiling as he walked with us across the mill yard, but his words and manner were civil enough.

"I am to take you gentlemen wherever you wish to be,' he said, in a deep, uninflected tone of voice, 'Show you whatever you wish to see."

Thoughtfully, I looked about me, and as thoughtfully approached the site of a disused well standing more or less at the yard's centre. "I say, Holmes," I called, pointing with my stick, "look at this." For it had just now occurred to me that this neglected hole in the ground might serve very well as a tomb.

Joining me at the few loose timbers that shuttered it, Holmes and I looked down. But all below was blackness, and it seemed a long time before a dropped stone struck a dry bottom. 'Twenty-eight feet" declared he, having made some abstruse calculation. "Give or take a few inches."

Even as we peered down, listening to the echoes, some loosened mortar fell, like a tiny avalanche, into the void.

"Take care, gentleman," Strickland cautioned us. "Yon well's to be filled in, and not before time. Captain Carrick's orders."

"Then the well has been plumbed?" queried Holmes.

"That is has. Sent a bobby down in a bucket, would you believe?"

"And found nothing?"

"Nothing but the bottom." Strickland came as near as maybe to smiling. "`Fill it in as soon as you like', says the superintendent of police to the Captain. `See to it, Strickland', says the Captain to me, `but wait for my say-so'."

"Quite right," confirmed Strap, sticking his thumbs behind his lapels and puffing himself up as if he'd given the orders himself. "A danger to man and beast that well is."

Pendleton in snow

It was foolish of me, of course, to think that the police might have overlooked so obvious a place, for they are nothing if not thorough in such matters. Yet there was in the manner of Sherlock Holmes that which suggested he had learned something of value. Rejoining the others, we made our way towards the mill-house, passing close to a water-wheel joined by a flume to a sluice grinning with icicles. In ordinary times all would be alive with sound and movement as the brimful lake beyond the sluice fed water to flume and wheel. Now the glazed paddles of the wheel and the beard of ice in the flume lay still and silent.

Guided by Strickland we made our way along a string of outbuildings, the door of each chalked with a cross indicating, so the farm manager informed us, that the interiors had been searched. Reaching the last of these, Strickland threw open the door and entered, telling us to wait while he lit an oil lantern hooked to a chain depending from the rafters.

"There you are, gentlemen," he announced, pointing to a long box-like object set on trestles, "this is the Great Candle you have no doubt heard about."

Drawing near, I saw that what I had taken for some sort of box was an open-topped mould made from fence timbers and that it was filled with unrefined tallow, grey-white and quite opaque. At the centre of one end of the mould there protruded through a hole bored in the wood what was obviously the wick, and with it, though much longer, two strands of thin wire, which I surmised were intended to guy the candle.

For his part, Sherlock Holmes was totally absorbed in the minutiae of our surroundings, poking and prying into every nook and cranny even, on one occasion, dropping to the dirt floor and sniffing at it. Then, springing up, he crossed to a bricked-round iron copper and kicked open the furnace door, releasing a fall of white ash. There was a trail of congealed wax leading from the copper to the candle-box, and more wax, also congealed, in the bottom of the copper; while lying nearby were two unused slabs of the stuff. Next to these were two metal swill buckets, one larger than the other, the smaller with hardened wax in the bottom. But it was the larger bucket that most exercised Holmes's attention, and we watched in silence when he upended it and turned out several lumps of partially burned coke and some ash.

"For our little museum of case relics, Watson," he remarked, tossing to me a lump of coke. "The ash I think we shall do without. Who fashioned the candle?" he added, addressing Strickland.

"The work was done by Old Mother Dempster and her cronies, with Mrs George looking in to supervise."

"You did not participate?"

"No, Mr Holmes, I did not."

"But you are the farm manager."

"Aye, and the farm I'll manage, but I'll have no truck with the likes of Alice George and the Dempsters. When orders came from the Hall to give them use of the copper, that's what I did. And that's all that I did."

"And none of your household or your workers was involved?"

"To the best of my knowledge they were not."

"Thank you, Strickland," said Holmes, "you have described the *mise-en-scène* and your own position most admirably."

So saying, Mr Sherlock Holmes led our little party outside, where I skidded on what felt like a patch of ice on the step, but which proved, when I kicked it free, to be a splash of dried wax. It was then, as I turned to close the door behind me, that I saw that Strickland had left the lamp burning ... and how like a coffin the candle-box appeared.

Catching up with the others, I was in time to see Inspector Indigo Strap remove his bowler hat and take from within a bread and cheese sandwich, which he commenced to bite into, and I confess that as well as regarding this episode with astonishment I did so with some degree of envy, aware that, given Holmes's disdain of food when immersed in a case, it was unlikely that he, and therefore I, should soon partake of any.

Following Strickland, we now commenced in a clockwise manner, to make a circuit of the mill lake, shortly coming to a shallow bay, its shape defined by a crescent of quite tall trees, the centremost host to a pile of broken masonry.

"Recently tipped," observed Sherlock Holmes, no doubt noting that the heap was free of snow. "And from the well-head, if I am not mistaken."

This was not so obvious, but Strickland at once nodded his assent. "It is to become a base for the candle," he explained.

"And this is indeed *un petit théâtre naturel*," approved Holmes. "Here where we stand is the stage; these trees are both backdrop and canopy, and there," he added, with an outward sweep of his arm, "there before us is the auditorium. Excellent! Quite Excellent! You are to be congratulated, Strickland."

"Oh, it was Miss Blaze picked out this spot, Mr Holmes."

"And the stand for the candle, was that her idea also? Or do I neglect a more practical mind?"

"That order came from the Captain," replied Strickland. "And now, gentlemen, if you will follow me, we shall see what more there is of interest."

Towards the top of the lake there were more trees. One of these, a drooping willow, grown so close to the bank that there was a bruised circle where the forming ice had gripped the tip of an outflung branch; all together not unlike a bowed rod and a taut line when there is a strong fish on the hook.

As we walked on and I imagined the scene to come - of

bright moonlight illuminating the weaving figures of skaters
enlivening a surface that at present looked merely blind and
staring and greyly translucent - instead of feeling uplifted I
experienced an almost visceral sense of dis-ease, generated,
I supposed, by the dead acoustics of the place. Where one
might have expected sound to be sharp and carrying, there
was a depressed, cotton wool effect that could not wholly be
attributed to the absorbent blanket of snow with which the
lake was girt.

My companions, however, seemed unaffected by the
atmosphere: Holmes puffing at his pipe; Strap wearing the
slightly smug expression of one having recently gratified the
inner man; Strickland striding purposefully ahead. Thus, in
our no doubt disparate states of mind, did we return to the
mill-house yard.

"It is already two hours after noon," declared Sherlock
Holmes, briskly, "and we must return Strickland to his
duties. There is no doubt much yet to do before the fair
tomorrow."

"Indeed there is," replied the farm manager, "for though
the fair is not until daygate (17), my part must be done with
well beforetimes. Yours, I fancy, will take a deal longer," he
added, before turning on his heel.

***

And so, eventually, back to Clitheroe and the friendly
warmth of the Swan and Royal Hotel, where Holmes and I
were joined at dinner by an expansive, not to say garrulous,
Inspector Indigo Strap; who first impressed and then amused
by consuming a main course sufficient for two men and
capping it with what he termed 'a mixed fruit compost'.

"We had a disappearing case some years since," he
volunteered. "Man by the name of Badger. Kept a piggery."

"What became of him?" I asked.

"Like I said - disappeared. Here one day, gone the next.

Clitheroe, the Swan and Lion Hotel is on the left of the picture.

Vanished from the land of the living. Just like Sir Giles Carrick. Rum."

This last word was directed at a passing waiter.

"What was your view of the matter?" inquired Holmes.

"Pigs. You know the saying, Mr H? You can eat all of a pig except its squeak. Well, for my money, a pig can treat a man likewise."

"But not, perhaps, his clothing."

"Aye, but a man can be stripped and his clothes burned."

"Look here," said I, as Strap poured onto his fruit compote half the gill of rum he had ordered, "surely you do not think that Sir Giles Carrick might have been murdered and fed to the pigs at home farm?"

"All I'm saying is what I think happened to Theodore Badger, Doctor Watson. But it were a long time since; I can't rightly say what I think this time round. But here am I answering all these questions; what about you, Mr H - what leads do you follow in this present affair?"

"Besides those I have brought to your notice, there is the matter of the two swill buckets and the several pieces of coke. Also the wax on the step of the outhouse. Oh, I have leads; it is in linking these leads to deeds where I am at an impasse."

"A guess, then?"

"My dear, Strap, I never guess. To do so is to embrace the random philosophy of the quack. Nor do I theorise. Sans data, truth occupies a void. Isn't that so, Watson?" insisted Holmes, turning his grey eyes upon me. "It is facts and facts alone that have substance. First the acquisition of facts, then the application of logic. Indeed, it is an invariable maxim of mine in such matters to apply the four protocols of Descartes." (18)

"The only carts I know," declared Strap, with a toothy grin, "have a horse in front."

"Then pray do not put the cart before it," advised

Sherlock Holmes. "And now, if you will excuse me, I think an early night is in order."

What I anticipated upon rising the next morning, simply on account of its being the second day of February and the date of the Candlemas celebrations, I do not quite know; only that what transpired during the forenoon and afternoon proved irksome in the extreme. I have rarely known Holmes so languid during a case. At breakfast he spoke and ate little, poking with a penknife into the bowl of this outlandish pipe of his and eventually stuffing it with shag apparently kept loose in one of his jacket pockets. This done, he abruptly declared his intention of visiting the telegraph office in order to send a wire to his brother Mycroft, and as abruptly departed.

Feeling somewhat piqued I retired to my room and settled down to write up my notes, which not unrewarding task occupied me until just before noon, when returning downstairs I found Sherlock Holmes engaged in conversation with a now agitated Inspector Indigo Strap.

"As if the police hadn't enough on our plate, Mr Holmes," he was saying as I approached. "Have you heard the news, Doctor?" he asked, turning to me. And before I could reply: "It's Driscol, the murderer. He is on the loose."

"And will no doubt soon be recaptured."

"Don't be too sure, Doctor Watson. Ewart Driscol is a homicidal lunatic, with all the cunning of his kind."

"You say he is a murderer?"

"Two local women, butchered like cattle."

"When was this?"

"Three and four years since."

"Then he was not apprehended the first time?"

"Like I say, Doctor; Driscol is cunning, and he was well hid."

"And you have no knowledge of his present whereabouts?"

Strap shrugged, more, I fancy, in irritation than despair. "He could be anywhere. Those as break out can break in."

"But the conditions," I persisted, "surely he will not get far, with the police and the populace at large on the lookout?"

"The police are stretched as it is, thanks to this Pendleroyd business. As for ordinary folk, they'd sooner avoid Driscol than look for him. Well, gentlemen," concluded Strap, making for the door, "I must get on, though whether to turn left or right I'm sure I don't know."

Following this brief but alarming interlude the afternoon developed much as had the morning, with Holmes setting off on some errand of his own and I first reviewing my notes and then adding to them the news about Driscol. This done, I drew an armchair up to my bedroom window, where I must have fallen asleep, for the next thing I knew was of a dark figure stooping over me, and a lean hand, claw-like in the gloom, plucking at my shoulder.

"Come, Watson, come!" cried Sherlock Holmes. "It is after six, and the game's afoot."

So saying, he bundled me into my outdoor attire and hustled me downstairs and into a waiting trap. Soon we were fairly rattling along our way lit by a waxing moon. It was cold, too, in the open trap, the night air pricking like the points of so many needles. Eventually, we turned into the narrow lane I remembered, and when we had travelled some little way down it there appeared, as if suspended in mid air, an all-black shape flapping and croaking like a ruffled crow. As we drew up, I perceived the apparition to be a man seated on a milk-white mare so perfectly blended with the snow as to seem part of it.

"Parson Tobias Catlow, I take it?" called out my companion.

"At your service," returned the other, in a harsh tone of voice. "The way is wider from here," continued Holmes.

"Perhaps we might converse as we travel on together?"

Tobias Catlow proved to be a beak-nosed cleric, with a sharp and bitter tongue. It was folly, he declared as he rode alongside the trap, this celebration; for was not Candlemas also the time when witches held their unholy sabbat? And would not the Devil attend the one and pervert the other?

Were the Prince of Darkness to gain sway, he ranted on, his cracked voice rising, there would be great wickedness abroad, with singing and dancing and drinking and debauchery; aye, and the touching of flesh out of wedlock. It was a prospect, he averred, to diminish all Christian men and women.

"Is this not so, Mr Sherlock Holmes?" he ended, in a voice of thunder.

"Whose part in all this vexes you most?" inquired Holmes.

"Miss Blaze Carrick is mistress of Pendleroyd, is she not? Who else am I to castigate?"

"Not Sir Giles, her father?"

"He, too, must bear the burden of fault; he who was steward of men's comings and goings hereabouts."

"As you have the cure of souls?"

"But am not the sole curate. Among his many accomplishments the Devil adopts that guise with consummate ease."

We left Catlow much as we found him, seemingly transfixed 'twixt earth and sky, his milk-white mare once more invisible before a bank of snow.

That Strickland, the home farm manager, had been hard at work was soon evident: the well in the mill yard had been fenced round, and signs illuminated by lanterns pointed the way to the lake, where more lanterns, raised on poles, marked its periphery. There were stalls, too, and glowing braziers offering roasted chestnuts and potatoes; and, of course, there were revellers, some on skates, tyro and adept alike laughing and calling. And at the edge of the lake, erect and unsheathed beneath its sentinel tree, stood the candle, a lozenge-shaped flame leaping in the frosty air. Quite eight feet high on its cairn the living obelisk invited our closer inspection, and as Holmes and I gingerly took to the ice to avoid the congested pathway we were joined by Rufus and Blaze Carrick in company with another couple.

Simon and Lydia Farthingale of Hodderholm Manor (19) - for this was who the couple proved to be - struck me as a well-suited duo: she bubbling with high spirits, twin dimples of amusement enlivening her peach-smooth cheeks; he large and booming, with protuberant eyes and a hearty laugh. Even Holmes appeared at ease, even to the extent of remarking upon our recent encounter with Parson Catlow.

"Whose pet passion," roared Simon Farthingale, "is that of a bigot exercising his dogma. The fellow is as unbalanced as a butcher's scales. As for the cure of souls he claims, it is my opinion that he could not cure a flitch of bacon!"

"Simon!" Lydia Farthingale hissed, affecting alarm. "We are already marked down as heretics, do you wish us burned as well?"

But he simply snorted and stamped ahead, drawing Rufus Carrick after him.

"Burning is an apt description of my present degree of curiosity," smiled Sherlock Holmes, taking up the conversation and diverting it.

"In what connection, Mr Holmes?"

"I am a keen student of phonology and am proficient in forty three regional intonations. Yours, I confess, baffles me."

"The Farthingales originate from Wem, in Shropshire."

"You choose to tease me, Madam."

"I do, and I apologize," she replied, frowning. "I am myself a Trevisick, as I suspect you may know; and the intonation you claim not to place is Cornish."

"Where the connection is one of admiralty?"

"Admiral Sir Jervis Trevisick is my kinsman."

"And what of this gentleman steward in your husband's employ - how is he named?"

"He is known as John Storm, Mr Holmes."

"Known as! Known as! Pray do not play games with me, Mrs Farthingale. The stakes are already very high and it would be unwise if by otiose point-scoring you were to raise them further."

"Mr Holmes," breathed the startled woman, her cheeks of a sudden blanched and her eyes wide and appealing, "I beg of you, not now! Not here! You and Doctor Watson must stay tonight at Pendleroyd Hall, as Simon and I are invited to do." And then, with a swift change of tone and manner such as Holmes himself might have contrived: "Why, though, here we are near the candle. I do believe humankind to be quite as foolish as the common moth. What do you say, Captain Carrick?"

But Rufus was gallantly making a way for us,urging aside with practised authority the crowd gathered before us.

"Good God!" boomed Simon Farthingale as we joined him and Rufus at the front. "Who the Devil is that perched on the wall beyond the candle? My thump, Carrick, I do believe it is that Humpty Dumpty housekeeper of yours."

Then another voice, sharp and urgent: "Look out, missus! Look out, I say!"

Whereupon Mrs Alice George brought together her knees and caught between them the missile she had evidently seen speeding towards her.

"Oh, well fielded, Missus," Indigo Strap congratulated her, thus identifying himself as the voice of concern and not that of the culprit. "A most foolish prank, that - whizzing a hot spud. They are not plentiful this year."

Strap's unblinking stare fixed on a nearby brazier, where a tray of the vegetables were baking. "You did not observe who threw it, I suppose? Never mind, you were alert when it mattered. More eyes than a seed potato, if you'll pardon the expression."

"Brats," Alice George grunted. "Over there." She paused from smoothing down her tentlike skirts of black bombazine and jabbed a thick finger towards some scooting youths. "Chucking at the candle, I expect."

"Very likely, missus." The Inspector picked up the badly squashed missile. "There's the villain of the piece - a half baked Ribble Valley Red."

Yet Sherlock Holmes, when I looked at him, was staring not at this entertaining by-play but at the brightly-burning candle, his aquiline features set in an expression of utmost concentration. Miss Blaze Carrick, too, appeared strangely affected, and she was to say later that the candle seemed to radiate not light but darkness. So potent was the sensation, and so unnerving, that for the space of one terrible moment she felt transported and glimpsed in her mind the maimed face of evil.

Silently now, we watched the molten wax run like lava down the candle's sides and over the stones heaped beneath it, and thence onto the glassy surface of the lake, where it rapidly congealed and blended remarkably with the underlying ice.

Looking sideways from the scene before me, my attention was caught and held by a face in the crowd. It was a face upturned in ecstatic contemplation of the soaring flame of the candle. The eyes, wide and cornflower blue, and the mop of flaxen hair, belonged to a girl of perhaps nineteen or twenty years. Beside her, as bent and thin as the other was straight and buxom, huddled an old woman. Yet there was a likeness, persuading me that these two were the Dempsters, mother and daughter.

Now the old woman was jabbering something into young Grace's ear, pointing the meantime at a gawky figure standing so close up to the candle that its spindly black-gaitered legs looked not unlike charred sticks thrust into the cairn. There was no milk-white mare this time to soften the impact; not this time the faintly ridiculous aspect of a ruffled crow. For a little while Tobias Catlow stood still and silent, head bowed as if at prayer. Then, as he threw back his head and the light fell on his face, I read there a contorted expression of the most awful anguish; as though what he witnessed constituted a dreadful blasphemy.

And as the crowd saw what he saw it delivered itself of a deep and atavistic, "Ahhh!"

"Bring torches! Fetch wood!" Rufus Carrick took command at once, and when, at last, the faggots had done their work and all the wax was gone, a skeleton, its bones picked clean, swung gently above the spent pyre.

Now Strap took charge, hoisting a willing youth into the branches of the gibbet tree and saying to Rufus: "I must submit both the wire and the bones to Doctor Braithwaite, Capting. He is the police surgeon and must be fetched to the mill house.If you will kindly---" But his last words were lost when the skeleton fell with a clatter at their feet.

Of all those who witnessed to its undignified end this obscene disrobing, and who heard the crowd's awed consensus that the skeleton was that of Sir Giles Carrick, or caught the muttering of the few who hinted at witchcraft, none could have been wounded as his daughter stood wounded, and it was my fervent hope that a merciful Providence had so blinded her eyes with tears that she had neither seen the glow of elemental rapture that transported the Dempsters nor the light of vindication that, as though from a nimbus, illuminated the face of Tobias Catlow.

"Go after her, Watson! There is a byway, steep but passable."

Realizing that the distraught girl had fled, I at once heeded Mr Sherlock Holmes's imperative and plunged after her. From the direction the path took I surmised it connected the Hall and home farm, and that Miss Carrick would know it well. I, of course, knew it not at all, and for all the moon was bright I soon found myself in difficulties, not least where the track was all but obliterated by fallen snow, or where it dipped without warning into treacherous declivities. In due course the way assumed a rising nature, and though I was well shod and had the support of my ash it required dogged work on my part to keep going. So engrossed was I in keeping my feet, that as I crested the summit of my climb and in so doing fell flat on my face, I became aware that I was no longer alone.

Below me, on a smaller plateau, I saw the stationary figures of Miss Blaze Carrick and a mounted horseman, and thus found myself in the invidious role of spy and eavesdropper.

"Where to, then, mistress?" The rider's question was peremptory.

"My destination is no concern of yours, sir," came the spirited answer. "Nor yours mine."

He laughed at her then, a young laugh and not unpleasant. Are you always so frosty, Miss Blaze Carrick of Pendleroyd? Or is your coolness as much a cloak for your doubts as is that cowl for your beauty?"

"So you have learned my name and marked my face. Am I the object of your esteem, or of your concern?"

"If conceit were wisdom, you would recognize the first and have less need of the second."

"And if impudence were breeding, you would pass for a gentleman."

The charged silence was broken by a faint snicker from the horse, and again when the brooding stranger said: "You have a sharp tongue, Mistress. Take care it does not blunt your other senses."

"It is Mr Farthingale's new steward, is it not?" she

71

hazarded. "And what advice have you, Master Steward? How to sit my horse when spied upon from afar? When to blink if dazzled by the flame of a candle? Where to look for my father?"

I was thus reminded of the conversation between Lydia Farthingale and Mr Sherlock Holmes, when he, too, had alluded to the coming of this gentleman steward. I thought also of the gleaming skull that had mushroomed from the dwindling candle, of bones like knotted string ...

"You are from the West Country, I believe," Miss Carrick continued. And when he neither agreed nor contradicted: "It is to be hoped you do not transport a grudge. One hears tell of fierce feuds and violent deeds in those parts."

She was mocking him, and his reply contained its own hint of banter. "You are too steeped in Blackmore (20). And see yourself as Lorna Doone, perhaps?"

"And what face do you turn to the world? Is it that of John Ridd, or of Carver Doone?"

"In real life, heroes and villains seldom look the part."

"You speak from experience, it seems?"

"If being schooled in the company of men and made a victim of their deceits exemplifies experience, then my 'prentice days are well attested."

"So you take issue with a woman!"

"And converse with a mule!"

As these last words were uttered and sank deep into the Carrick pride, she slapped hard at the horse's flank. "Either lead or follow, but pray give me passage."

"Then I shall provide safe escort to Pendleroyd," he declared. "Nor shall I be far from there later, should you have need of me."

"You may be as far away as the North Pole, for all I care!"

And as he wheeled his horse and swept off his hat in

mock obeisance I saw his face, and read in it an expression I could not then fathom. Then a dark cloud crossed the moon, and when it had gone the plateau was empty.

Getting stiffly to my feet I set off the way I had come, and eventually arrived back at home farm to find a small coterie of officials occupying the mill house kitchen. Present authority, it transpired, was vested in Inspector Indigo Strap, who presided over an assemblage of bones on an otherwise empty table; bones so free of flesh and sinew that they gleamed ivory-white; bones, moreover, which were neatly drilled and wired together.

It was at once clear to me such gleaning could not have come about by natural causes. The articulation of the joints was another factor in the puzzle, carried out with wire noticeably finer than that employed in suspending the skeleton. This, I perceived, had been effected by threading two wires - those I had assumed to be guys - upwards through the skull.

Of a sudden one of the skeleton's hands fell with a rattle down the side of the table, punctuating some banality uttered by Strap and heralding the arrival of an extremely tall, thin man, with a face like a much-used palimpsest, with the kind of whiskers known as Dundreary Weepers (21). As he came, stooping, through the door he screwed a glass into one eye and looked about him. "What, you here, Catlow?" The voice was as dry as old parchment. "You, too, Strap? My word, if the Devil cast his net what a haul he'd make! Well, it had better be important. I was at my victuals when the constable came. Ah, what's this? What's this?"

'This' was the skeleton, which by dint of screwing the monocle into alternate eyes the good Doctor commenced to examine.

"Er, could you certify death, please?" inquired the police official.

"Don't be daft, Strap."

73

"It's procedure," insisted Strap, drawing himself up. "And an approximation as to the time of death."

"About one hundred years ago, I should think."

"As long as that?" Strap sounded impressed. "May I ask how you can be so exact, Doctor Braithwaite?"

The Doctor produced what passed for a chuckle. "This is Hippocrates, Inspector," he explained, replacing on the table the skeleton's fallen hand; "my anatomical soulmate from my student days. Haven't seen him for years. He lives in a cupboard in my study. Must have got out!"

"Taken out," growled Strap. And to me: "Good of you to attend, Doctor Watson, but we shan't require a second opinion. Nor," he added, grimly, "the services of a consulting detective to apprehend the culprits."

But where is Sherlock Holmes, I wondered, realizing that he was not present. And what, for that matter, had become of Rufus Carrick and the Farthingales. Fortunately, Doctor Braithwaite was as anxious to return to his supper as was I to divest my wet clothing, and he kindly conveyed me in his trap to Pendleroyd Hall, where, to my profound relief, I found a full complement of `missing persons' and a cordial, if understandably subdued, welcome.

***

Notwithstanding the alarums and excursions of the evening and that I retired to a strange bed, I fell almost immediately into a deep and dreamless sleep, which, being so, rendered me unaware either of the passage of the hours or of what transpired therein.

Suffice to say that I awoke all of a piece, as I had become conditioned to do when bivouacking in Afghanistan. Now as then I came to with every nerve pricked, the salient senses of sight and hearing acutely alive. What had brought me to this condition of rapid awareness, I did not at first comprehend, for I could hear nothing save the sound of my

74

own heart; see nothing beyond the end of my nose. Then, as I was about to fall back on the pillow and put my sudden awakening down to a subconscious reaction to recent events, I distinctly heard the closing of an outer door, followed by the sound of gravel crunching underfoot.

Leaping from my bed, I crossed to the casement and threw it open, witness to a scene such as I had never before experienced and never again hope to do so. At the centre of the driveway, where it widened without the portals of the Hall, was what I at first took to be a single, grotesque figure, but which quickly delineated into two: a giant of a man, whose footsteps I had heard, and slung athwart his massive shoulders, not so much like a human form as a bolster dragged carelessly from a bed, the limp and crumpled figure of a young woman. That I was seeing Driscol, the escaped lunatic, and that Miss Blaze Carrick was his hostage, I knew instinctively; just as I knew that were I to call out the madman might make use of the knife he was carrying. Had he done so already I could not tell, for though the moon was yet strong and its luminescence bathed in a clear light the dreadful scene below me, it was not possible to see if the knife was bloodied.

Still I remained at the casement as if rooted there, some words of Indigo Strap revolving like a mantra in my otherwise shock-stilled mind. "Those as break out can break in," Strap had said of Driscol. And this is what he had no doubt done, gaining entry into Pendleroyd Hall during the household's absence at the fair. Whether his choice had been at random or had been in some way dictated by those same great lunar influences that move the oceans, only an alienist might say. All I knew was that it had happened. Driscol had got in, had marked down his intended victim, and had remained hidden until, in the dead of night, he had crept unseen along a silent corridor and opened a certain door ...

The sound of another door opening and closing - and this

nearby - brought me to my senses, and in one convulsive movement (or so it seemed) I snatched up the dressing gown I had been loaned, thrust my feet into slippers from the same source, and bore downstairs in the wake of a figure I recognised as that of Mr Sherlock Holmes.

Never has a corridor seemed so long, or a flight of stairs so steep; nor a front door so heavy. But at last Holmes and I found ourselves on the other side of it, there to find that the drama had taken another turn. Miss Blaze Carrick - for it was she - lay supine on the gravel, as though dropped or thrown there, while close by a cloaked and booted figure was in the act of falling. Even as Holmes and I ran forward, another figure, squat and swarthy, appeared, and at the end of a shambling run reached up and fastened both hands about Driscol's neck.

That the newcomer was Mrs Alice George and that she was fully dressed did not then excite my interest. Overriding all else was the realization that she now stood toe-to-toe with Driscol - he towering head and shoulders above her, she perhaps the broader of the two - and that they were locked in mortal combat.

To record that it took the combined strength of Sherlock Holmes and me eventually to bring the conflict to an end would be no more than the truth, notwithstanding that the life forces driving the protagonists were rapidly draining from them; Driscol's by reason of strangulation, Mrs George's following the many stab wounds she had sustained.

As first one and then the other sank to the ground, I turned to the still form of the girl. "Thank God, she's all right," I cried, upon kneeling beside her. "And this fellow," I added, helping to his feet the Farthingale's gentleman steward.

"I promised to be on hand," he castigated himself, 'should she have need of me."

"And so you were," I assured him, not daring to reveal

that I had eavesdropped on that promise. "You must not reproach yourself. The blow you took would have felled an ox, and in sustaining it you may have saved a life."

By now the entire household was awake, and placing Miss Carrick in the care of servants attended by a solicitous young man with a lump on his head, I returned to where Sherlock Holmes knelt between the bodies of Driscol and Mrs George.

"He is beyond the help of man," announced Holmes, indicating the *petechiae* (22) suffusing the whites of the madman's bulging eyes.

"And Mrs Alice George is dying," I replied. "The knife wounds are many and deep, and ... Holmes!" I cried, in a voice I scarcely recognized as my own.

"What is it, Watson?"

"Holmes!" I repeated. "It is ... it is Mrs George ... she is ... Good God, Holmes! Mrs George is a man!"

"Oh, yes," said he, carelessly. "I have known that for some time."

"You knew! How?"

"By her manner of catching a hot potato."

"Which, as I recall, she did between her knees."

"Precisely. That is the manner in which you or I or any man would endeavour to catch such a missile, while a woman..."

"Would do so by spreading her skirts!"

"Admirable, my dear Watson. Your choice of words is as vivid as some of the titles you have succumbed to when chronicling our little adventures. Ah, Captain Carrick, you have arrived at the close of a rather hectic quarter of an hour. Perhaps if we step inside you will be good enough to summon Inspector Indigo Strap and Doctor Braithwaite."

"Mrs George ..?" murmured Rufus Carrick, hanging back.

"Is dead," I informed him. "Your niece, I am happy to

say, is alive and well; as is the young man."

As we made to re-enter the Hall, I plucked at Holmes's sleeve. "Mrs George," I whispered, as yet unable formally to recognize the change in gender, "she uttered a few words."

"I did not hear them."

"They were barely audible."

"But you understood them?"

"I heard them; I did not say I understood them."

"Then pray repeat what you heard but did not understand."

"Ding-dong-bell," said I, feeling somewhat foolish. "I fear the woman was rambling. It is not unusual in such cases."

"Ramblings or a dying deposition?" mused Sherlock Holmes. "Well, we have broken stiffer ciphers than that. But for the time being let us join the others and await the arrival of Strap and Doctor Braithwaite, if only to see the look on the face of the latter when he learns that his is not the only skeleton in a cupboard."

Strap and the Doctor arrived together and, while the first entered into a private discussion with Sherlock Holmes the second divided his time between ministering upstairs to the living and attending downstairs to the dead. Of the Farthingale's mysterious gentleman steward there was no sign, though Simon Farthingale - for once reduced to a comparative whisper - had just now appeared, his wife apparently having stayed to comfort Miss Carrick.

"It will be dawn in less than an hour," I heard Strap say to Holmes. "Do you and Doctor Watson go there ahead of me, I will see to matters here and then follow. Oh, by the way, Mr Holmes, this wire came for you care of the police office."

"I was expecting it," replied Holmes, stuffing the buff envelope into his pocket. "It is from my brother Mycroft, and though the contents will no doubt prove factually of interest

78

they are, by now, bound to be corroborative rather than informative." And then, addressing me *sotto voce*: "Well, Watson, if you are willing to forgo the rest of your sleep and to partake of a scratch breakfast, I should welcome your company at home farm."

Thus it was (our having at Holmes's insistence endured the rigours of the back way from Pendleroyd Hall) that in due course we emerged close to the place where the candle had stood, and where nothing remained save a trodden bed of wax and a few scattered stones. It was, however, to a spot some way from here, almost to the top of the mill lake, that Holmes led, there to reach out and shake the willow branch I had the other day likened in my thoughts to the bowed rod of an angler. But now, the rod of my imagining hung without tension, its tip clear of the ice. Yet the ice was as I remembered it: bruised and solid, lacking only the captive tip of the willow; or, to perpetuate my imagery, the taut line occasioned by the pull of a fish.

Even as I watched and pondered, Sherlock Holmes stepped on to the frozen surface of the lake, where he proceeded first to kneel and then to dig with the blade of a jack-knife. Soon it was apparent that what he was removing was not ice but wax, and eventually, by cutting and stabbing at its periphery, he was able with my help to remove a roughly circular piece some twenty-four inches in diameter.

It was not until Holmes turned his attention to the end of the redundant willow branch that the silence between us was broken. "As you observe, Watson," he remarked, as a much out-of-breath Indigo Strap burst upon us, "the tip of the branch is quite badly mutilated; and here, if I am not mistaken, are some hempen fibres. You do well to appear dumbfounded, Strap, for these are the trappings of devilry far beyond that ever practised by the so-called Pendle Witches."

"Holmes," said I as we regained the bank and started towards the mill, "does this mean the willow was used as a tether, with the body of Sir Giles Carrick on the end of it?"

"You suppose correctly, Watson."

"Then his body has broken free, and we must endeavour to retrieve it."

"Oh, tut! How then does the tether come free also, while leaving intact the wax plug? For make no mistake, Watson, that is what it was, not once but twice, a wax plug - a *trompe l'oeil.*" (23)

"Got it, Mr Holmes," broke in Strap, still puffing from his exertions. "You-know-who does for Sir Giles, ties him to yonder willow branch and pushes the body under the ice, having already cut a hole in it. Then the same party - or should I say parties? - lets the bottom of the hole ice over before topping up with wax."

"Brought in a swill bucket from the copper-house," supplemented Holmes.

"But surely the wax would have hardened between locations?" I protested. "It is a fair way from the copper-house to the top of the lake."

"It is indeed," agreed Holmes, "in which connection I would again draw your attention to the ash and the spent coke cinders found in the copper-house."

"But they were in a second swill bucket."

"Into which the small bucket fitted."

"Like a glue-kettle," contributed Strap. "In this case, with a coke fire in one bucket and wax in the other, the job might be done in two trips. Talking of trips, Doctor, I fancy you slipped on some of the spillage on the copper-house step."

By now we were getting closer to the mill house, and as though by tacit consent we lowered our voices. There were as well sounds other than ours, but of a sort I could not place or identify, only that they were some way ahead of us.

"You said just now," I reminded Holmes, "when describing the wax plug as a *trompe l'oeil,* that it was employed twice?"

"The device, yes; but not, I think, by means of the same plug. No, no, the first would have been too damaged. In all probability the placement of a second plug was undertaken in the early hours of this morning, when the fish had been landed."

"Good Lord, Holmes! You mean Sir Giles's body has been withdrawn from the lake? But why? And what has become of it? And what brings you to this conclusion?"

"I should have thought," responded Sherlock Holmes, as we approached the line of outbuildings leading on to the mill house, "the answer to the first question is self-evident. Ice melts, does it not? and it would never do to have Sir Giles Carrick's body fetching up at the sluice. As to your second question, it is my intention, with the official assistance of Inspector Strap, shortly to reveal the present whereabouts of the missing knight, and in so doing to expose the workings of a most ingenious and diabolical conjuring trick.

"Concerning your inability to grasp the logic of my deductions, I will say only this: if on one day I observe a frozen-over lake, a small area of which has embedded in it the tip of a willow branch, and on another day I observe the same small area without the tip of a willow branch embedded in it, I am forced to conclude either that the branch has broken free or that the small area of the frozen-over surface I am observing has changed in some way. But here we are at the copper-house. Do you go inside, Strap, we shall soon know the outcome of my hypothesis."

"Just as we suspected, Mr Holmes," smirked Strap, upon emerging. "The furnace is still warm, there is soft wax in the bottom of the copper, and both buckets have been in use. What is more, he added, tapping with a thick finger the side of his long nose, "a certain party has left in some dross the print of a boot."

"Excellent, Strap! Excellent!" approved Holmes. "You have the makings of a first class detective officer Now if you will take the lead, I think we might bring this part of the affair to a conclusion. There is no risk of our being interrupted, I take it?"

"None whatsoever, Mr Holmes," declared Strap, striding forward. "I have posted constables at all the approaches, including the back way. More will join us at my signal."

The jumble of sounds I had heard earlier were explained when, upon rounding the corner formed by the last of the string of outbuildings, our little party debouched into the mill yard, where Strickland, the farm manager, was supervising several labourers shovelling into the disused well lumps of masonry I had last seen used for a cairn.

While clearly surprised at seeing us Strickland did not seem in any way alarmed, stating that he was carrying out instructions given to him the night before by Captain Rufus Carrick.

"Had we arrived somewhat earlier," remarked Sherlock Holmes, not unkindly, "you would have been saved a good deal of trouble. As it is, the masonry you have deposited must be retrieved. "You see, Watson," he explained, turning to me, "this is the finale to the conjuring trick I spoke of. First a demonstrably empty well ... next a *trompe l'oeil* concealing the body of Sir Giles Carrick ... followed by a *trompe l'oeil* concealing nothing ... finally the use of the well as a tomb."

"Remarkable," said I.

"Rudimentary," said he.

Remaining only long enough to satisfy ourselves that there was in fact a body in the well and that it was that of Sir Giles Carrick, Holmes and I begged a ride in the police trap returning for Doctor Braithwaite. At the last moment, Strap climbed in too.

"Recovering bodies is no work for a first class detective officer," he grinned. "My place is with the owner of that boot print. You will see I get due credit, Mr Holmes?"

"You shall have the credit for that, and more," Sherlock Holmes assured him. "My reward lies in the elucidation of a complex and seemingly insoluble mystery. I am to Justice what a finely drawn bow is to a Stradivarius."

Breaking in on these self-congratulatory exchanges, I pressed Holmes about the individual I continued to think of as Mrs George.

By way of answer, he first patted a pocket of his Inverness and then commenced, in that succinct and sometimes didactic way he has, to impart intelligence which, though fascinating in itself, seemed to have no bearing on the question I had put to him.

"I have received from my brother Mycroft (24) details of a court-martial to do with the misappropriation of imprest funds aboard one of Her Majesty's warships. There were two officers arraigned; the Captain of the vessel, who was exonerated; and an acting paymaster-lieutenant, who was found guilty, largely on the testimony of the Master-at-Arms, a chief petty officer.

"The outcome was not, however, considered wholly satisfactory. There was talk, some at high level. According to Mycroft, who is, of course, privy to such deliberations, it was made pretty plain to the Captain that he would go no higher, whereupon he resigned his commission. A short time later, the disgraced ex-imprest officer, who had returned to the family home in the West Country, suddenly disappeared from that locality; the Chief Petty Officer just as suddenly deserting his ship.

"I need hardly add, that the name of the ex-ship's captain is Rufus Carrick, and that of the cashiered officer is Adam Trevisick, known to us as John Storm. I have it from Mrs Farthingale, that young Trevisick, with her contrivance and that of her husband, took up residence at Hodderholm Manor, ostensibly as a gentleman steward, in the hope of compromising Rufus Carrick and in some way of

83

establishing his own innocence in the matter of the imprest account."

Throughout this quite lengthy exposition the police trap had proceeded at little more than a walk, the surface of the lane being worse rather than better for the recent traffic it had sustained. As a consequence, we were yet some way from Pendleroyd Hall, and I determined to discover before we arrived there all that remained dark to me.

"But Mrs Alice George?" I persisted, harking back.

"Is - was - one *Alec* George," divulged Holmes, "the witness whose evidence at the court-martial cleared Rufus Carrick and implicated Adam Trevisick; and who, armed with knowledge which would reverse the positions of the two ex-officers, followed Rufus Carrick to Pendleroyd Hall and blackmailed him into providing a haven and an income."

"But why the masquerade, Holmes? Could not Alec George have been taken on as a manservant rather than as a housekeeper?"

"You forget, Watson, that Alec George was a deserter from the Royal Navy, and, were he to be apprehended, he would be harshly dealt with."

"This is all very well, Mr Sherlock Holmes," commented Indigo Strap, adopting, to my way of thinking, an insufferably waggish way of speaking, "but it seems to me that you suspected something amiss with the Capting and this George before you heard from your brother?"

"You are no doubt alluding to the time of her arrival and the sounding of the factory hooter at Chatburn," acknowledged Holmes. "It is my recollection that the two happenings coincided, yet the timetable of the Yorkshire and Lancashire Railway Company is void of any related passenger train arrival. A straw in the wind, Strap, but one suggesting Mrs Alice George, as she had by then become, was come from somewhere nearer than Manchester and that Rufus Carrick was privy to the deception.

"From that moment on," continued Holmes, as the trap came within sight of Pendleroyd Hall, "these two would become inextricably linked in a *folie à deux*, for it was Rufus Carrick's intention to dispose of Sir Giles Carrick, his brother, and so, eventually, to inherit what by the law of progenitor had hitherto been denied him."

"But without a body," I ventured, anxious to elicit facts in their entirety, "would that not have taken some time?"

"Indeed it would?" agreed Holmes, "but Rufus Carrick could afford to wait."

"And if Sir Giles had made an overriding provision in favour of his daughter?"

"In that event," returned Sherlock Holmes, grimly, "I fear there would soon have been another death at Pendleroyd."

"Good God, Holmes!"

"Do you doubt it?" he demanded, betraying the outraged emotions of the good and compassionate man I knew him to be. "Already these two had struck down the girl's father; already these two had twice boiled candle wax in the dead of night; already they had consigned a frozen body to a deep-sunk well; what, then, should stop them now?"

"And the skeleton in the candle?" I urged. "What significance lies in that?"

"None," replied Holmes, shrugging, "beyond mischief-making by the Dempsters and their cronies, the settling of which we may safely leave to Parson Tobias Catlow and Doctor Braithwaite. In all likelihood Rufus Carrick and Alec George knew what was afoot, and did little to discourage it."

"And Strickland?"

"Is, I believe, an honest man; if an incurious one, so incurious that he was unaware that Sir Giles Carrick's horse had been stabled overnight at home farm."

"Well," I remarked, leaning inboard while the police trap turned through the gates of Pendleroyd Hall, "it would seem the surprises are over for one day."

Clitheroe Castle, seen from the rear window of Watson's brougham.

But in this I was quickly proved wrong, for the moment we vacated the trap Inspector Strapp pulled strongly at the bell, and, upon gaining admittance, led us without ceremony into the room we had quitted some hours earlier, and where all were sharing a constrained silence.

Without hesitation the police official came to a halt immediately in front of Rufus Carrick. "Capting," barked Strap, "please be so good as to stand. No, no, Capting, it won't do to argue. That's the ticket. Now, if you will kindly turn about and raise your right foot ..."

Whereupon Strap performed, for me at least, the second conjuring trick of the morning. Reaching down with one hand and up with the other - or so it seemed so quickly were the movements executed - he took from under his bowler hat a flattened piece of wax which he pressed against the upturned sole of Rufus Carrick's boot.

"A perfect fit, Capting," declared Strap, "proving to my satisfaction that you were in the copper house at home farm sometime between the hour of midnight and four o'clock this morning, when you and an accomplice did by divers means seek further to conceal the body of Sir Giles Carrick, this being contrary to common law. Now, then, Capting, if you will just put your foot down and your flippers out, I'll put the darbies on. Mr Holmes, it has been a pleasure to work with you."

Upon which masterful note Inspector Indigo Strap replaced his bowler hat and marched out his whey-faced prisoner.

It was some time later, when Holmes and I were seated in a first-class smoking-compartment of the parliamentary train taking us on the first leg of our long journey home, that I again raised the subject of Mr Alec George.

"You know, Holmes, had it not been for him, Miss Blaze Carrick would in all probability have been slain."

"The labyrinth that is the human mind has not yet been

fully mapped, Watson," my friend replied, commencing to charge his pipe. "Sometimes, where we anticipate good, we encounter evil; and vice-versa. It is my conviction, that upon perceiving Miss Carrick's life hostage to the lunatic Driscol, there emerged within the recent chief petty officer a surge of decency which impelled him to forfeit his life for hers; and in so doing he, in part, redeemed himself."

And still something nagged at the back of my mind. And as our train began the curve taking the line into Blackburn, it came to me. "Those dying words of his, Holmes - Ding-dong bell..."

"Ding-dong bell, Pussy's in the well ... It seems to me, Watson," remarked Mr Sherlock Holmes, putting a flame to his pipe, "that as well as a sense of decency, Mr Alec George had a sense of humour."

EPILOGUE

Some time after the events I have sought to chronicle, Holmes and I learned, respectively from Mycroft Holmes and from Indigo Strap, that the court-martial findings on Adam Trevisick had been quashed, and that the young man is these days much seen in the company of a certain young lady.

Footnotes

(1)   William Foggitt, the Yorkshire Weather Man, has it in his grandfather's records, that 'The winter of 1895 was extremely severe, particularly in February, when here (at Thirsk) the temperature was $11.2°F$ below average'.

(2)   The London physician who had purchased Watson's small Kensington practice. The chronology of the canon suggests that the sale was in the summer of 1894 or 1895.

(3)   Then (and now) the principal market town of the Ribble Valley.

(4)   Covering a wide area of Pendle Hill and its sweeping lowlands, the place names of Sabden, Fence, Newchurch, Barley and Roughlee are perhaps the most apposite, the Clitheroe side of the Hill being somewhat less troubled.

(5)   There were two main families of witches, that of Elizabeth Southern, alias Demdike, and that of Anne Whittle, alias Chattox, and between which there was deep and abiding enmity. Among the more colourful names these so-called witches went by was that given to Demdike's daughter, Elizabeth Device, who was known as Squintin' Lizzie.

(6)   A village north-east of Clitheroe and almost contiguous.

(7)   The journey then from London to Preston was by the LNWR (London & North Western Railway), departing Euston at 10 am, arriving Preston Fishergate at 2.20 pm. Onward travel from Preston to Clitheroe, via Blackburn, would have been on the Lancashire & Yorkshire Railway, the scheduled connections for which were: Dep Preston 2.55 pm, Arr Blackburn 3.55 pm; Dep Blackburn 4.28 pm, Arr Clitheroe 4.57 pm.

(8)   The Great Hill of Pendle, or more simply Pendle Hill, lies between the cotton towns to the south of it and the rich farming lands to the north, and rises to a summit of 1831'.

(9)   Padiham, Burnley, Nelson, and Colne, a string of towns now, if not then, contiguous. No longer associated with mill chimneys and the 'clatter of clogs'.

(10)   Observed as a church festival in commemoration of the presentation of Christ in the temple and the purification of the Virgin Mary; the candles blessed and carried in celebration.

(11)   There are four great festivals: Candlemas (2nd February); May's Eve (also called Beltane or Walpurgis Night); Lammas (1st August); and Hallowe'en (31st October). These dated, more exactly than our equinoxes and solstices, the beginning of the seasons.

(12)   Actually Indigo and not Inigo, presumably in the hope (if not the expectation) that Strap would make his mark on the world!

(13)   Its walls and Norman Tower are perched on a high limestone rock, and though the Castle cannot be said to dominate the town of Clitheroe (it is too small for that), it is nevertheless a landmark, particularly as seen on the approaches from Whalley and the west.

(14)   Briefly and starkly put, many, indeed most, of the so-called Pendle Witches were carted off to Lancaster Castle, incarcerated in the dungeons there, tried at the Summer Assizes, and hanged. Demdike, however, pre-empted the hangman by expiring from natural(?) causes.

(15)   The hey-day (if it may be called such) of the Pendle witches was in the years before their arrest, which was in 1612, in the reign of James I & VI, himself an 'expert' in the matter of witchcraft, and the author of a book _Dæmonologie_ published in Edinburgh in 1597 and re-issued in England in 1603. There were two great purges of witches; that of 1612 (which saw off Demdike and Chattox and a host of others) and that of 1634, when Jennet Device, Demdike's granddaughter (and a kind of

super-grass at the earlier trial) was herself arraigned and, with others, tried and hanged.

(16)   Not as described anywhere in the canon, but widely assumed elsewhere. It is intriguing that, denied his Persian slipper, Holmes should use the pocket of his jacket as a pouch for his loose tobacco

(17)   An old word meaning, literally, the gate closing after the day. Sometimes used in the longer form of Daylightgate.

(18)   René Descartes (1596-1650) French philosopher, who, in his treatise *Discours de la Méthode* published in 1637, set out the four protocols 1. Never accept as true anything that cannot clearly be seen as such; 2. Divide difficulties into as many parts as possible, 3. Seek solutions of the simplest problems first and proceed step by step to the most difficult; 4. Review all conclusions to make sure there are no omissions.

(19)   No doubt taking its name from the River Hodder, Hodderholm Manor thus lay to the west of Pendleroyd Hall but within easy riding distance, probably in the vicinity of the village of Chaigley.

(20)   R. D. Blackmore's classic novel *Loma Doone*, set in the West Country.

(21)   A pair of whiskers cut sideways from the chin and grown long. Generally antiquated by 1882 and distinctly unfashionable by 1892. But not, it seems, in the Ribble Valley.

(22)   Tiny pin-point haemorrhages in the whites of the eyes and in the cheeks, symptomatic of manual strangulation.

(23)   To deceive the eye. A device used in painting, sculpture, architecture and the like achieved by optical illusion. A popular *trompe l'oeil*, now passé, was to paint an open door onto a high garden wall so creating the illusion of another garden beyond.

(24)   Sherlock's senior by seven years, Mycroft Holmes ostensibly audited the books in certain Government departments, but in fact, in the words of his younger brother, Mycroft occasionally *was* the British Government.

The Case of the Missing Masters

"It is good of you to come so promptly, Mr Holmes. And you, too, Doctor Watson. I cannot say how relieved I am that you have consented to look into the problem that besets us."

"Not at all, Major Shuttleworth-Brown," replied Mr Sherlock Holmes, shaking hands with the tall, soldierly-looking gentleman who had come down the platform to greet us. "The nature of your letter prompted me to travel to Ripon by the first available express."

"I am delighted that you did so. That to which I referred remains unresolved, and I am commissioned to extend every facility in your seeking to remedy the situation. But here is my carriage," the Major added, ushering us through the ticket-barrier and into a four-wheeler. "In the half hour it takes to reach Granby Lodge, I shall endeavour to state more fully the facts of the matter."

"Please have the goodness to do so," assented Holmes as our conveyance turned on to a bridge spanning a swirling river (¹). "Watson here knows nothing of what has passed."

Which statement was the absolute truth, for having plucked me willy-nilly from my practice and then dragooned me into a mad dash to catch the afternoon flyer out of King's Cross, Mr Sherlock Holmes had hardly opened his eyes or his lips until we were rattling across the great Crimple viaduct on the outskirts of Harrogate.

Keeping me in ignorance both of our eventual destination and the purpose of our excursion, he had upon our reaching the spa fairly bundled me out of one train and into another, with the terse comment that if the second proved as punctual as the first we should arrive at the ancient city of Ripon, some dozen miles up the line, at 6.54 pm (²).

"As I said in my letter," resumed Major Shuttleworth-Brown, "the burglaries took place on successive nights. The first was on Monday, at Craige House, the home of Sir Giles and Lady Wheeler; the second was at Taplow Hall, the seat of Lord and Lady Guthridge. In each instance entry was effected directly into the room in which the painting hung; that is, into the library and the drawing-room respectively."

"Was the frame as well as the canvas taken?"

"On both occasions, Mr Holmes, though I am given to understand that the frames are cumbersome and of no intrinsic value."

"Hum! So far we have heard what happened on Monday and Tuesday. Today is Friday, I am agog as to what took place on Wednesday or Thursday?"

"But nothing took place on Wednesday or Thursday, Mr Holmes."

"Dear me, then the plot is even deeper than I had imagined, for I am right in thinking, am I not, that you, too, are the owner of a painting of some merit?"

"It is a minor Rembrandt."

"Forgive me, but it is necessary that I should know its approximate value."

"My painting is worth several thousands of pounds on the open market."

"And to the collector?"

"Who can say?" shrugged the Major, frowning at this line of questioning. "I believe that sometimes the mania knows no bounds, either of price or principle.

"No one has approached you with a view to acquiring the Rembrandt?"

"No. Nor would I contemplate selling it. The painting has been in my family for a great many years."

"Quite so. No doubt Sir Giles Wheeler and Lord Guthridge entertain similar sentiments in regard to their works of art, and, like you, would not hesitate to discourage a prospective buyer?"

"I should be surprised if the necessity has arisen."

"Oh, pooh! Such bids may be made so obliquely as to pass unremarked."

"Be that as it may," countered Major Shuttleworth-Brown, "the point is surely academic. My friends' homes have been violated and the paintings stolen."

"While yours has not."

"True. But then, as an old army man, Mr Holmes, my defences are possibly more secure. Since the break-ins, I have had my grounds patrolled day and night by armed men."

Instead of congratulating our companion on taking what seemed to me an admirable course of action, Holmes stared silently out of the carriage window, apparently absorbed in the passing scene.

"Are the missing paintings Rembrandts also?" he asked eventually, returning his attention to the Major.

"The Wheelers' is a Reubens; the other is a Van Dyck."

"Excellent!" cried Sherlock Holmes, clapping his hands together with such gusto that we gaped at him in astonishment. "The common factor which one looks for in cases of this kind is more subtle than I had supposed."

"Should this be a matter for our satisfaction, Mr Holmes?"

"Certainly. There is nothing so dull as the predictable. Depend on it, Major Shuttleworth-Brown, were the evidence one whit less challenging I should forthwith return to Town. As it is, please be so good as to say if anything particular strikes you in regard to the Reubens and the Van Dyck."

"Only their inclusion in the Cunningham Portfolio."

"The name means nothing to me; please be precise as to details."

"Oh, it is to be a limited edition of privately-owned Works of Art, selected by Mr Sylvester Cunningham (³), and reproduced by him by means of the collotype process at his printing works in Ripon."

"This is most illuminating, commented Holmes, leaning forward in his seat. "Should you now say that the Rembrandt also features in the collection, I am bound to conclude that the Reubens and the Van Dyck share some other distinction that the Rembrandt does not."

"My word, Mr Holmes!" gasped Major Shuttleworth-Brown, "I do not know how you have come by such esoteric knowledge, but you are absolutely right in your supposition. You are alluding no doubt to the visits paid to Craige House and Taplow Hall by the Chevalier Gaston Moulinard, *Maître* of the Paris Louvre.

Sherlock Holmes sank back with every outward sign of satisfaction. "You know my methods, Watson," he smiled, glancing in my direction. "Let us hear what you deduce from the facts that have so far been presented."

I must confess that there have been some few times, when my friend and I have been engaged on a particularly difficult case and he has at some point thrown it open to my interpretation, when I have essayed a solution that has proved to be somewhat wide of the mark. On this occasion, however, so confident was I of having grasped his drift that I had no hesitation in saying: "Plain as a pikestaff, Holmes! The Reubens and the Van Dyck were taken by this Chevalier fellow!"

"On what basis do you reach that conclusion?"

"On the basis that he called on Sir Giles Wheeler and on Lord Guthridge."

"Really, my dear fellow!" remonstrated Sherlock Holmes, chuckling into the collar of his Inverness, "I do believe that you would as readily accuse the Archbishop of Canterbury! Nevertheless," he temporized, "I should like to know a good deal more about Chevalier Moulinard's activities. Ha! we are turning off the road. Perhaps there is time before we reach Granby Lodge?"

"Certainly, Mr Holmes," responded Shuttleworth-Brown,

adopting the clipped, no-nonsense delivery that I had become used to during my spell in the Army Medical Service, "events are so recent that I have it off pat ..."

Apparently the Chevalier was known personally to the Wheelers and to Lord and Lady Guthridge, and had availed himself of the opportunity afforded by an official visit to York - where he was to appraise some pictures belonging to the Minster - to stop off at each of his friends' residences, calling at Craige House on the Tuesday and remaining there overnight, and then repeating the arrangement at Taplow Hall on the Wednesday. He had subsequently continued his journey to York, and was presently lodged in that city.

"Capital!" enthused Sherlock Holmes, when the Major's résumé came to an end. "Were the Chevalier's intentions widely known?"

"The local press carried his itinerary prominently enough."

"As *Maître* of the Louvre, he is presumably an acknowledged expert on various works of art?"

"The foremost in Europe."

"And is a collector in his own right?"

"He is a connoisseur, Mr Holmes."

"The terms are not mutually exclusive, Major."

"I believe he indulges a modest passion in that direction."

"What a pity he was not able to see either the Reubens or the Van Dyck. If I have correctly understood the calendar of events he was, in racing parlance, pipped at the post at each venue."

"The Chevalier was disappointed, naturally, but his greater concern was for the outraged feelings of his hosts. Indeed, he at once undertook to telegraph should either work appear on the continent."

"How considerate," murmured Holmes, putting the flame of a match to the cherrywood he had just now finished tamping. "Do I take it that you yourself are not intimately acquainted with *le preux chevalier?* And did not invite him to Grandby Lodge?"

"I am not and did not."

"And the local press did not speculate on that score?"

"Not as far as I know."

"But you had met?"

"We were introduced by Lord Guthridge."

"Capital!" cried Holmes, drawing strongly at his pipe, "you are in a position to furnish a description of the gentleman. He is something of the dandy, perhaps?"

"On the contrary; he is most conservative, both in his dress and his demeanour."

And so the dialogue continued, until Holmes terminated it with the words: "You are to be congratulated on all counts, Major Shuttleworth-Brown. Your account has materially strengthened the hypothesis I am developing. But here we are at your front door. If you would be so kind as to show me the Rembrandt, I hope soon to advise on a course of action that will ensure its safe-keeping, and which may very well lead to the recovery of the Reubens and the Van Dyck."

Soon Holmes had his nose almost touching the canvas of a small but quite heavily-framed painting of a Dutch polder. In a manner that was at once subtle and vividly realistic, the artist had captured the precarious impermanence of land lately wrested from the sea, and which, it was somehow suggested, might easily be regained by it.

As my friend continued to scrutinize the hanging, even to the extent of taking out his pocket-lens, I wondered how it was possible for him, such was his proximity to it, to appreciate the perspective of the work. Or to absorb its vitality, even though at first sight the subject appeared passive. Eventually, however, he concluded his study of the obverse, and turning the picture over commenced an examination of the back.

Meantime, Major Shuttleworth-Brown told me how he

The Unicorn Hotel, Ripon.

had come to consult Mr Sherlock Holmes, when it might appear that others were more directly involved. The explanation lay in the fact that when the Reubens and the Van Dyck were stolen, Sir Giles Wheeler and Lord Guthridge had formed such a poor opinion of the official police that the Major had recommended that the gist of the matter should at once be communicated to Baker Street, which proposal had appealed equally to the victims of the thefts and to the harassed officials charged with bringing to a conclusion an investigation they had no idea how to commence.

Returning the Rembrandt to its original position on the study wall, Sherlock Holmes said abruptly: "If you will instruct your man to return Doctor Watson and me to Ripon, Major Shuttleworth-Brown, we should arrive there in time for a late dinner."

"I had hoped that you would dine here, Mr Holmes?"

"It will suit my purpose better to do so at the Unicorn (4). We are, as you know, putting up there."

"Very well, I will give the necessary instructions. Also that should you decide to come here at any time, you are to be given safe passage."

"Oh, perhaps I did not make it clear," replied Holmes, striding towards the door. "Your patrols may be stood down. It is my opinion that the painting is in no immediate danger."

II

"Well, Holmes," I ventured when we had seen off some choice Wensleydale and were lingering over the last of a tolerable bottle of claret, "and what have you mapped out for us tomorrow? Interviews with Sir Giles Wheeler and Lord Guthridge, I expect?"

"Then your expectations are misconceived," said he, in his brisk way. "There is no data that they can provide that I

The
Horn Blower,
Ripon.

Ned Howard, Horn Blower from the turn of the century until 1917.

have not so far gleaned. No, Watson, my plans are altogether more positive. Indeed, should they eventuate in every particular, the outcome will enable you to blow my trumpet more loudly than the Wakeman (5) is presently sounding his horn outside the windows of the hotel. Always supposing," he added, with a twinkle in his eye, "that you should decide to chronicle this little adventure."

"But what of the police, Holmes?" I persisted, refusing to be drawn on the thorny subject of my writings, "surely you will be conferring with them?"

"I think not. By all accounts, they do not know how to proceed in the matter, even though the perpetrator of the crimes has made a most serious mistake. I refer to that concerning the Rembrandt."

"But the Rembrandt has not been stolen."

"That is the serious mistake."

Baffled, I steered the topic into what seemed more fathomable waters. "I thought the subject powerful without being obtrusive," I ventured, lighting a cigar. "What is your opinion, Holmes?"

"I did not form one."

"Oh, come now! You must have remarked the unique manner in which the artist has captured the atmosphere of the polder?"

"My dear Watson, I could no more say whether the paint on the canvas depicts a Dutch fen or a vase of tulips!" (6)

"But you examined the work minutely, even to the extent of employing your lens."

"Which shall shortly become the practice of every police agent," digressed Holmes. "The time is not far off when the use of the magnifying lens and the comparison microscope will revolutionize the detection of crime throughout the civilized world."

The next morning, however, it was at once apparent that he had left his visionary dreams on the pillow and was again applying his remarkable powers to our problems of the moment, for when I came down to breakfast it was to find him up and eager to be off, "Come along, Watson," he urged, fidgeting like a thoroughbred at the tapes, "if you can make do with toast and coffee we shall be in time for our appointment with Mr Sylvester Cunningham."

Careless of my digestion, he was soon hurrying me into my hat and coat and past a corner of a market place busy with tradesfolk setting up stalls. Proceeding down Kirkgate, we bore left of the Cathedral down Minster Road and turned right into Agnes Gate, coming in short order to some premises by the river. It was evident that Holmes had been out and about while I still slept and that he was expected, for upon rapping with his cane on a plain door, it was opened so abruptly inwards that he almost struck the face of a tall, gaunt man whose stiff yellow hair seemed to stand like corn stalks above the green crescent of his eye-shield.

"Sylvester Cunningham," he greeted us, in a curiously hollow voice. "At your service."

"This is my friend and colleague, Dr Watson," responded Holmes suavely. "It is good of you to agree to showing us over your printing works. We can no doubt see something of the process for which you are justly famous, and possibly find the time also to discuss the recent scurrilous happenings in the neighbourhood."

It occurred to me that Cunningham had in all probability agreed to nothing of the sort, but such is Holmes's affable guile when he chooses to employ it that only an exceptionally astute man or a churlish one may deflect him.

With a slow nod, the Master Printer conducted us into his inner sanctum, the upper half of one complete side of which consisted of narrow columns of glass panes over-looking a large workshop divided by means of head-high partitions into compartments, each communicating with the next through gaps left in the walls.

'... out of the Unicorn and along one side of the market place, which at nine o'clock was already thronged with tradespeople...'

"This is my eyrie," explained our host, waving us into seats. "From this vantage I can obtain a general view of my premises, or I an able to concentrate on a particular part of it. The exceptions are the camera room and my own studio, which are in another building."

"Your workers do not resent the intrusion?"

"Not in the slightest degree. I see and I am seen. A less honest man might paint these windows black and observe through a Judas hole, but that is not my way. But please say how best I may assist you in your inquiries?"

"By saying which of the originals intended for reproduction in the Cunningham Portfolio reached you first."

"The Van Dyck. I received it from Lord Guthridge a little under six months ago."

"How long did you keep it?"

"Six or seven weeks."

"And the Reubens?"

"Arrived after the Rembrandt."

"The Rembrandt, then?"

"Came when the Van Dyck was returned."

"And was kept?"

"Six or seven weeks also."

"When you returned it to Major Shuttleworth-Brown, and took charge of the Reubens from Sir Giles Wheeler?"

"That is correct."

"For a commensurate period of time?"

"The collotype means of printing cannot be quantified, Mr Holmes (7). It is undeniably the most exacting of the reprographic arts, and one which demands the utmost patience and expertise at every stage."

"Just so. I am merely attempting to establish an accurate chronology of events. If I have succeeded, the last of the three originals was returned to its owner between five and six weeks ago."

"Which signifies what, Mr Holmes?"

"That unless the portfolio is to contain only three plates, a fourth original has been received by you and is presently on the premises."

"That is not quite the case."

"Oh? In what respect is my reasoning at fault?"

"Not your reasoning, Mr Holmes; rather your arithmetic. I am currently working on a fifth subject. Mr Jerome K Studebaker's painting took up very little of my time."

Knowing Sherlock Holmes as I do, his rejoinder was deceptively casual. "Jerome K Studebaker, you say? That does not strike me as being a North Country name - or even English."

"Mr Studebaker is an American gentleman of my acquaintance."

"I see. This last picture, then. Perhaps we might be privileged to inspect it?"

"I regret that will not be possible. When Mr Winterbourne's Van Gogh is not on my retouching table, it is in the strong-room."

"I quite understand. Your mention of retouching interests me greatly. The work is carried out on the photographic negative, is it not?"

"Yes, it is the task of the retoucher to compare the negative with the original and to correct any discrepancies."

"Which work you execute yourself?"

"Without exception. I am the sole arbiter of the fidelity of the negatives that go forward for exposure to the sensitized printing surfaces. There is, of course, a different negative for each colour employed on the press."

"But the retoucher works only in shades of black and white, I believe?"

"That is so."

"Which must prove irksome in the extreme," commented Holmes. And before the other, who had become quite animated in his responses, could reply: "In like circumstances

I should be tempted to paint a picture of my own, in the most vivid of colours. Perhaps you are similarly inclined, Mr Cunningham?"

"Any spare time of mine is spent in the development of a revolutionary printing plate, and on a press to utilize it(8)."

"Revolutionary, you say?"

"In the most literal sense. Think of it, Mr Holmes! A plate so thin it may be flexed round an impression cylinder and rotated at high speed. When my patents are granted I shall be in a position to dictate terms to every collotype printer who wishes to employ my method of reproduction."

"That is indeed a glowing prospect," acknowledged Sherlock Holmes. "By the by," he added, rising, "I gather that Chevalier Gaston Moulinard, of the Louvre, is returning to Ripon. I happened to overhear a message to that effect delivered at the Unicorn. He arrives there this evening."

As we strolled back the way we had come, Holmes interrupted his humming of the Hoffman Barcarole to exclaim: "Well, out with it, Watson! That you have some dramatic conclusion to share is written all over your face!"

"Oh, it is nothing very much," said I, attempting the airy manner that Holmes himself adopts on occasion; "merely that as well as his other undertakings, it appears that Mr Sylvester Cunningham operates one of the printing presses."

"Which you have deduced from the stains on the thumb and index finger of his right hand?"

"Well, yes," I admitted, a trifle deflated by the readiness of this perceptive response. "There was the least fleck of yellow on the nail of the thumb, and a smear of vermilion on the end of the finger."

"Bravo, Watson! Your powers of observation are coming along by leaps and bounds. Yellow and vermilion, eh? Is that all? Well, never mind, here we are at the Cathedral. I am told the crypt was built for St Wilfrid in 672, and that there are some rare treasures on display."

III

Notwithstanding his earlier expressions of confidence in his ability to bring the investigation to a speedy conclusion, Mr Sherlock Holmes became manifestly more tense as the day progressed, until by mid afternoon, when we were seated *vis-à-vis* in the residents' lounge of the Unicorn, he could contain himself no longer.

"Well, Watson," he rasped, glaring at me over the tea cups, "what would you say if I were to abandon this case, and leave things to you?"

"I should say that you had taken leave of your senses," I retorted, conscious of the sideways glances our raised voices were attracting from people nearby. "You cannot possibly..."

"Pray do not tell me what is not possible. It is surely within your capacity to tie up a few loose ends?"

"I think there is rather more to it than that, Holmes. So far I have received no inkling as to the direction of your suspicions."

"Nonsense! You have been at my elbow every inch of the way." Then, with one of those swift changes of mood that is part of his complex personality, he produced a comradely smile and asked of me, "Will you take on the job if I swear that it is necessary, and if I reveal to you the plan I have evolved for the apprehension of the guilty party and for the recovery of the paintings?"

"I am game for anything, Holmes," I assured him. "You may rely on me to carry out your orders to the letter."

"Good old Watson! The litmus test never fails. Now listen carefully ..."

For the next few minutes Holmes spoke very rapidly, keeping his voice low and his face close to mine. "Remember, Watson," he adjured finally, "whomsoever leaves Granby Lodge after the household has retired for the night is to be intercepted and detained - by force, if need be."

"On what grounds?"

"The grounds will be self-evident."

"And if they are not?"

"At best we shall have made fools of ourselves, at worst laid ourselves open to criminal proceedings."

Upon which sombre note Sherlock Holmes abruptly rose and stalked out, leaving me to ponder on what had transpired and, belatedly, to realize that I did not have the least idea who my possible prisoner was likely to be. With this thought pulling at my mind, I whiled away the hours as best I might until it was time to go down to dinner, which I was about to order when a not-unfamiliar voice addressed me.

"Good evening, Doctor," Mr Sylvester Cunningham began. "I wonder if I might have the pleasure of joining you? Or is this empty chair reserved for Mr Holmes?"

I assured him that it was not, and requested that he be seated. "My friend has some pressing business elsewhere," I explained, "and has left me to my own devices."

"Nothing of an unpleasant nature, I trust? Now, if you have not made a choice already, may I recommend the roast pheasant? It is invariably good at this time of the year. And to follow?"

"To follow," said I, recalling the delights of the local cheese, "I shall have the Wensleydale."

As the meal proceeded I found myself studying Mr Cunningham with considerable interest, for outside his working environment, and minus his green vizor, he seemed an altogether more agreeable individual,

"You evidently know the kitchen here," I remarked when the bird had come and had proved to be as good as he had predicted. "Are you then a regular diner?"

"Yes, it is my one indulgence. I am a bachelor, you see, and I have developed the habit of coming here each night by

`... I stepped out of the hotel and engaged the first cab in line...'

way of convenience and relaxation." And then, appraising a newcomer to the dining-room: "It seems that Mr Sherlock Holmes was well informed. The gentleman in the celluloid collar is the Chevalier Moulinard. He appears rather full of his own importance, don't you think?"

"He is certainly full of something," I agreed, observing the plumpish figure squeezing in a corner table.

During the remainder of the meal, I found my perception of the Frenchman becoming increasingly anti-pathetic, for although his formal dress and reserved manner conformed with the impression created by Major Shuttleworth-Brown, there was that about the Chevalier that made me think him smug and self-centred. It had, perhaps, to do with the avid brightness of the narrow-set eyes glinting over half-moon spectacles perched part way down a long, fleshy nose, which in turn surmounted a prissy mouth and a pear-shaped chin; and that the long silver hair pulled into a queue at the nape of the neck invested him with an air of superior, almost feminine, elegance.

"There sits a discriminating man," murmured Sylvester Cunningham. "I hear that he intends visiting Granby Lodge, to view the Rembrandt."

"What, at this time of night?"

"Not until tomorrow morning. I do not mean to be disparaging, but Major Shuttleworth-Brown's table is known to be Spartan. Well, Doctor Watson, I must thank you for your most congenial company. Possibly we shall bump into one another again. Please give my regards to Mr Sherlock Holmes." So saying, my companion shook my hand and departed, passing close to the Chevalier and exchanging with him some few words of acknowledgment.

In due course, having donned the warmest attire I could muster, I stepped out of the hotel to the rank opposite and engaged the first cab in line. When, at last, we arrived at the gates to Granby Lodge, I paid off the driver and made my way into the grounds and thence into a summer-house, the door of which stood open. Making myself roughly comfortable on the seat within, I settled down to what I hoped would not be a fruitless vigil - or a lengthy one. Both expectations dwindled with the passing hours, for the house lights continued to burn in several ground-floor windows until half-past midnight, when, one by one, they were extinguished, only to be succeeded by others in the upstairs rooms. Eventually, these too went out and the sudden darkness brought with it the realization that in these Stygian conditions it would be quite impossible for me to intercept anyone escaping the house. What did not then occur to me was that the night was uniformly black for my potential adversary, and that he would be in need of a lantern. Indeed it was one shining from the direction of the road that next alerted me, setting my heart thumping against my ribs as the beam approached and then passed me by.

Now all was dark again ... and silent, and it must have been twenty or so minutes later when the splash of light reappeared, coming rapidly back the way it had gone. Soon it was abreast of me. In seconds my quarry would reach the gates. Gripping my stick, I charged out of the summer-house and collided with the figure behind the lantern, but before I knew what I was about something hard and angular hit me on the temple and I pitched headlong upon the grass.

Then, just as it seemed that all was lost, every light in the house came on, and there followed the sound of men running and shouting, and, from near by, the unmistakable voice of Sherlock Holmes saying: "Picture frames are so cumbersome, are they not? How unfortunate that you are burdened with one ... Oh no, you don't, Mr Sylvester Cunningham! I warn you that the arm-lock I am applying can be made exceedingly painful."

"Holmes!" I gasped, scrambling to my feet and staring at them in the glare of half-a-dozen lanterns. "Where on earth did you spring from?"

"Spring is hardly the word," said he, relaxing his hold of the prisoner while retaining a firm grip on the rectangular object he had evidently wrested from him. "I arrived by means of the same vehicle as our friend here."

"What, you shared a cab?"

"Well, not quite. You see, in order to keep Cunningham and the driver in ignorance of my presence I was forced to ride somewhat precariously between the back axle and the underside of the conveyance."

"We are in ignorance of much more than that, Mr Holmes," came a plaintive voice I recognized as belonging to Major Shuttleworth-Brown. "When you sent word that I was to expect a burglar, I did not for one moment suppose that he would turn out to be Mr Sylvester Cunningham."

"The element of surprise is never more shocking than when it involves a so-called pillar of respectability," replied Sherlock Holmes. "But pray let us continue this conversation indoors. The early mornings can be somewhat chilly, even at this time of the year.

"You may as well hang the cause of this little excitement back on the wall," he resumed when we had gained the Major's study, "even though it is quite valueless."

"What's that? I do not understand you, Mr Holmes!" The bewildered landowner stared at the painting he held. "How can its value have changed in the space of a few minutes?"

"It has not done so since I saw it two days ago. You see, Watson," Holmes continued, turning his keen gaze to me, "the stains you spotted when we interviewed Mr Sylvester Cunningham were not, as you supposed, the residue of printing inks but of the more heavily pigmented colours used for painting in oils. The yellow ochres and the vermilions are notoriously persistent (9)."

He switched his attention to the seated prisoner, who now that he had recovered from our recent skirmish seemed reconciled to whatever fate awaited him. "You have a God-given gift as a copyist, Mr Sylvester Cunningham, and your scheme to obtain certain Works of Art, ostensibly to reproduce in your Portfolio but actually to replace with facsimiles, was undeniably brilliant. Unfortunately for you, the two men in all England who could declare your work false came to this part of Yorkshire within a few days of one another. (10)

"One of whom is the Chevalier Moulinard," muttered Cunningham. "It was a black day for my aspirations when he chose to visit two of the great houses that were the recipients of my handiwork."

"And an even blacker one that I should visit a third."

"Oh, come now, Mr Holmes! You are without peer as a consulting detective, as your *coup* tonight amply demonstrates, but to put yourself up as an art critic..."

"Is to mistake my meaning. My expertise is of another kind; it is to do with observation and deduction. To the discerning eye the warp and weft of machine-made fabric is unmistakable. Had you been there, you would have noticed that I paid most attention to the back of the painting."

"But look here, Holmes," I put in, "why would someone in Cunningham's situation set out to commit such a fraud?"

"Precisely because he is in that situation, Watson. He is an overly ambitious man, and one who seeks to dominate the field in which he works. He is completely wrapped up in the idea of a novel kind of printing plate and the development of a fast press for the collotype method of reproduction, the pursuit of which aims has no doubt proved extremely costly; the patent fees alone may be quite staggering. Is it not tragically clear that faced with these harsh realities this resourceful, single-minded man conceived of disposing of as many minor masterpieces as need be, and, save two, has done so with each subject lent for the Portfolio, itself a potential source of future income.

"It is my opinion," continued Holmes, "that the receiver is wealthy dilettante, one whose own painting is featured in the collection. Oh, pray do not be alarmed, Major Shuttleworth-Brown, there are no more local reputations to be tarnished. The collector I have in mind is Mr Jerome K Studebaker, of America."

"How can you say so?" I demanded, stung into sharpness by the unexpected denunciation, and, truth to tell, by the throbbing of my bruised temple. "He is a rank outsider."

"As a sporting man, Watson, you should know that an outsider not infrequently comes into the reckoning. Does it not strike you that of all the originals handled by Mr Cunningham only Studebaker's was kept for a very short period? I suggest that the American's painting was not long kept because, unlike the rest, it did not serve as a model."

"I still cannot believe that this is a dud," marvelled Major Shuttleworth-Brown, holding his 'Rembrandt' at arms' length and submitting it to an intense scrutiny. "It corresponds exactly with the little gem I have looked upon each time I have entered this room. Yet if it is all as you say, Mr Holmes, why should not the thief have cut the picture out of its frame, and so made his task lighter?"

"Because, as I have just now indicated, an expert can detect new canvas; no less the remainder of one."

"Yes, yes, I see that. You have made everything crystal clear, Mr Holmes. There is, however, an aspect of the situation that I should like to discuss with you in private. Perhaps we might withdraw for a few moments?"

"That will not be necessary," replied Sherlock Holmes, commencing to fasten his Inverness. "If, as I surmise, it is to do with the fact that to bring a prosecution against Mr Cunningham would be to proclaim to Society that he has duped several of the Riding's most influential landowners, then I must tell you that my silence is contingent upon his meeting certain conditions."

"Name them."

"The restitution of the four originals to their rightful..."

"Four?" interrupted the Master Printer, cocking his head.

"Four," asserted Holmes. "You will recall that I said you had counterfeited all but two of the originals that had so far come into your possession. It would not do to omit Mr Winterbourne's Van Gogh, at present in your strong-room. The other three - the Reubens, the Van Dyck and Major Shuttleworth-Brown's Rembrandt - you will retrieve, by whatever means, from Mr Studebaker."

"I shall oversee the transaction," promised Major Shuttleworth-Brown. "What else do you have in mind?"

"That should the cheat and swindler who now sits before us break his parole in any particular, you will see to it that he suffer the full rigour of the law."

"You have my word and my hand, Mr Holmes."

Whereupon Mr Sherlock Holmes fixed the wretched Master Printer with a compelling stare, and said: "When next you aspire to see and be seen, Mr Sylvester Cunningham, be sure that it is an honourable man your audience beholds ... and not a worthless imitation."

Later, as we sat back in the window corners of a first-class smoking compartment, Holmes inquired of me whether it was my intention to chronicle our little adventure, and when I said that it was, "Under what heading?"

"I shall call it The Case of the Missing Masters," said I. "I think you will agree, Holmes, that the title is most apt."

"On the contrary, it is my opinion that the play on words is both meretricious and inaccurate."

"Surely not! You cannot deny that Chevalier Gaston Moulinard, *Maître* of the Paris Louvre, was absent from the scene of action earlier this morning, or that you yourself did not arrive until the very last moment."

"Nevertheless, Watson, in the event of your putting pen to paper I shall hope for a more factual superscription."

"I must say, Holmes," I replied, a trifle nettled by his didactic manner, "that you are as severe on my literary endeavours as you have been lenient in the extreme towards Mr Sylvester Cunningham."

"Hum! So that is your conclusion? And I had formed an impression that you had taken a shine to the fellow."

"Nothing of the sort! I simply said that we passed an enjoyable hour together. It is hardly my fault that he made a bee-line for me."

"My dear Watson, grand theft, as our American friends call it, is a serious undertaking. Our man had to be sure that the Frenchman was in fact resident at the Unicorn, and joining you for dinner was the best way of keeping watch."

"Well, he was deuced glib about it - spun me no end of a yarn."

"I am sure that he did. Really, Watson! I am not aware that I have said something of an amusing nature?"

"Sorry, Holmes! I was just thinking of Cunningham's words as we parted following dinner last night. He said: 'Perhaps we shall bump into one another again.' Deuced funny, when you consider what happened later."

"Excruciating!"

"You are right about his keeping tabs on Moulinard, though. He even spoke to him on the way out. You know, Holmes, it was jolly fortunate that this French johnny should turn up when he did, and with the declared intention of going on to Granby Lodge the next morning."

"Extremely."

"I wonder what he made of it all when he got there?"

"If he got there," murmured Sherlock Holmes. And for a moment, as the train rattled on its way, and the grassy slopes of a cutting rose up on either side, the face opposite mine seemed to swell and change form, even to the extent of a fleshy nose and a pear-shaped chin. Then, in the time it took our compartment to pass beneath the arch of a stone bridge, the illusion was gone, and there remained only the familiar countenance of my old friend, albeit with a smile on his lips and a twinkle in his eye.

Footnotes

1. The River Ure. North Bridge joins Hutton Bank, on the Thirsk side of the river, to North Road, on the Ripon side.

2. Watson is in error. While there was c.1900 a service from London to Ripon: depart King's Cross 1.30 pm, arrive Ripon 6.54 pm, the change was made at Holbeck. It was not until comparatively recently that there has been a through service from King's Cross to Harrogate.

3. There is no record of a Sylvester Cunningham living in or near Ripon at this time, nor were there residences known as Granby Lodge, Craige House and Taplow Hall. However, it would not be the only time Watson has thought fit to change personal and place names.

4. The Unicorn Hotel faces the east side of the market square, at the top of Kirkgate.

5. The individual Holmes refers to as the Wakeman is the Ripon Horn Blower, the last Wakeman having died more than two centuries before. It is the task of the Horn Blower, at nine o'clock each evening, to blow his horn at each corner of the market square, a custom known as Setting the Watch.

6. Vindication, surely, of Watson's contention in one of his other writings (HOUN) that Holmes had only the crudest ideas of art.

7. The collotype process was then the only commercial method of reproducing full tone originals - watercolours, oil paintings and the like - without the use of a photo-mechanical screen.

8. The standard collotype printing plate was made of glass, and owes its development to Joseph Albert, of Munich, who called his prints Albertotypes. It was not until 1963 that the first flexible aluminium plates appeared and were allied to relatively high-speed rotary methods of printing.

9. Collotype printing inks and the pigmented colours used when painting in oils are, respectively, of a low and high viscosity. In printers' terms, a collotype ink is known as a 'short' ink.

10. Some people have the gift of being able to copy precisely the work of others.

The Case of the Singular Sibling

"You know, Watson," remarked Mr Sherlock Holmes, observing from the window of our sitting-room the world at large, "there is something about the calm that follows a stormy night that is uniquely soothing to the spirit. Sadly, though, the sensation is of but passing duration, for there soon develops a natural vacuum that in due course another storm must fill. So it is with criminal folly; no sooner is one act accomplished than it is succeeded by another."

"To err is human," I murmured, from my seat by the fire.

"And to forgive, divine?" He half turned toward me, so that his strong, hawk-like features appeared in sardonic profile against the window glass. "Even when the error encompasses great wickedness? I do not consider that Alexander Pope intended the aphorism to be interpreted quite so liberally as your response presumes. It is my opinion that were there a hundred consulting detectives, our concerted efforts would not eradicate the tide of evil that daily threatens the populace at large and that to postulate universal forgiveness is to impose upon society a burden beneath which it must eventually stagger and fall."

"I say, Holmes, steady on!" I protested, coming from behind my *Times*, and regarding him in some astonishment. "If this is the effect upon you of a howling wind and a wet chimney, it is fortunate that we are not domiciled in Shropshire. According to a report here, the county has had its worst December deluge in living memory."

"Really?" said he, evincing a bare modicum of interest. "Then let us hope that we are not required to go there (¹) But pull up another chair, Watson, so that our visitor may share the hearth."

His quick ear had evidently registered the arrival of someone below, for the words were scarcely uttered than there came a tap at our door, which opened to admit the housekeeper closely followed by a tall, heavily-veiled woman.

"I am Mrs Vincent," she announced, in a deep, though not un-melodious voice, when Mrs Hudson had departed. "Here to consult with Mr Sherlock Holmes."

"I am he," said Holmes, remaining in the window space. "I do not recollect your having made an appointment to see me, Mrs Vincent."

"That is because I have not done so," she returned coolly, throwing back her veil to reveal firm, almost hard, features. "But when you are better acquainted with my identity and have heard what brings me to Baker Street, I am sure you will overlook the omission."

Frowning, Holmes bade Mrs Vincent be seated, then threw himself petulantly into his armchair. "Then please be as brief as possible," he instructed.

"My maiden name was Shelagh Moriarty," Mrs Vincent informed us, "and I am the sister of the late Professor James Moriarty, whom I know to have been your sworn enemy." (²)

I can honestly say that in all the years that I have known Mr Sherlock Holmes, I had never, until this moment, seen him gape at a client in utter stupefaction. That he did so on this occasion bears witness to the impact of the claim our informant laid before us.

"I am also the wife of Mr Bartholomew Vincent, of Oswestry," she continued. "You may recall that a year ago he was sentenced to a long term of imprisonment for embezzling funds deposited with the Shrewsbury and District Bank. My husband has always denied the charges brought against him, and, three days ago, he escaped from Chester Prison. According to the police, he has gone to ground in, or in the vicinity of, Krihc House."

"Which I surmise is your place of residence?" interpolated Sherlock, his composure now somewhat restored. And when the other indicated that this was so, "The official police are usually to be relied upon in such matters. I really do not see in what capacity I may be of assistance."

"You may restore to me my peace of mind, Mr Holmes!"

"How?"

"By returning with me to Krihc House, and by demonstrating to the police that my husband is not concealed there. Inspector Roscoe Brick and his men have not given me a moment's respite since Bartholomew broke out."

For several seconds the only sounds were from the street below, where the usual mid-morning bustle was in progress, and it was plain that there was about this grave, determined woman and her story that which Sherlock Holmes found of compelling interest.

"Very well, Mrs Shelagh Moriarty Vincent," he said at last, "if I am to be of service, I must first put to you certain questions."

"I shall answer them to the best of my ability."

"Where is Krihc House located?"

"It is in Shropshire, five miles to the north of Oswestry, near the village of Chirk."

"Chirk is in the county of Denbigh (^{3}), is it not?"

"That is so, but the house is just on the Shropshire side."

"The location is obviously a rural one."

"And quite isolated, especially at this time of the year. Our only visible links with civilization are the Great Western Railway and the Welsh Canal, both of which pass through our land, the latter from Llangollen, a few miles within the Principality."

"The canal is clearly in evidence, then?"

"From the upper windows of Krihc House it may be seen all the way to Chirk Bank, and in the other direction until it leaves the southern portal of Chirk Tunnel. There it is possible to see a section of the railway line also, where it and the waterway run side by side."

'... a wretched passage along lanes so dark and narrow, and so damply overhung with foliage, that our conveyance seemed to slither down a serpentine tunnel of unremitting gloom...'

"Thank you, Mrs Vincent, you have depicted that part of the canvas admirably. Now let us consider Krihc House. Do I understand that the police have executed a search warrant?"

"They have looked everywhere."

"And have discovered nothing?"

"Nothing more than the echo of their own prejudice. Inspector Brick is in many ways a decent enough man, and I cannot think why he chooses to persecute me in this way."

"Well, Watson," responded Sherlock Holmes, leaping to his feet, "you were saying just now that Shropshire has had a soaking. By all accounts a storm of sorts still rages there. Let us hope that upon our arrival its most singular nature does not blind us to the truth."

To record that our journey was an enjoyable one would be at variance with the facts, for after driving pell-mell to catch the late morning train from Paddington, (4) the next few hours were spent for the most part in an uncongenial silence. At long last, however, the railway fly was setting us down without the closed door of Krihc House, which we had reached after a wretched passage along lanes so dark and twisting, and so damply overhung with foliage, that our conveyance seemed to slither down a serpentine tunnel of unremitting gloom.

"You do well to keep your windows tightly shuttered," approved Sherlock Holmes, addressing Mrs Vincent when we had been admitted to the house. "The police are posted in some strength."

"I did not see any sign of them," said I.

"They are there nevertheless, Watson," said he. And then, as there sounded a hearty rat-a-tat-tat on the panel of the door through which we had just entered: "That, if I am not mistaken, is a police official come to see how the land lies."

Police Inspector Roscoe Brick of the Shropshire Constabulary's Detective Department - for this was who the newcomer, a youngish, well set-up man wearing canvas

"I have raised a levy of special constables for this duty - farmers, gamekeepers and the like."

leggings and a corduroy cap, proved to be - came to the point as briskly as the manner of his knocking might suggest.

"It is Mr Sherlock Holmes, is it not?" he inquired cordially, removing his cap. "Our people informed me of your arrival, Mr Holmes."

"You are to be congratulated upon the accuracy of your information," responded Holmes, shaking the local man by the hand. "And upon the rapidity of its transmission."

"Oh, we"re pretty well up to the mark here, you know. You were tagged all the way from the railway station."

"I am aware of that. I observed your men signalling by means of their lanterns. (5) How many officers have you deployed, by the way?"

"There are around fifty of us."

"Dear me, the law-abiding citizens elsewhere in the county must feel somewhat neglected."

"Not at all," retorted the Inspector, laying a thick finger along his nose. "I have raised a levy of special constables for this duty - farmers and gamekeepers and the like - so no one need be any the worse off. Except for the fellow we're after, of course! In my view, it is impossible for him to evade our cordon."

"You see no weakness in it?"

"If you are alluding to the Welsh side, Inspector Lloyd Williams is co-operating in every particular, even to sharing a motor tricycle the better to patrol the boundary separating the two forces. But see here! Just to show that we provincials intend to play fair with you London gentlemen, why not join me in a tour of these premises?"

"This is insupportable!" protested Mrs Vincent, plucking at the sleeve of Holmes's Inverness. "They have ransacked the house on three previous occasions."

"The warrant still runs," said Brick curtly. "Well, what do you say, Mr Holmes?" And when my friend acquiesced: "I will call in twenty of my men. That is the number of

... even to sharing a motor tricycle, the better to patrol the
boundary separating the two forces...'

rooms there are, and I will station a man in each of them."

Whereupon Inspector Roscoe Brick summoned a posse of constables, and thereafter conducted Holmes and me on a room-by-room itinerary of Krihc House, with poor Mrs Vincent bringing up the rear. Upstairs and downstairs we went, through this door and that, sometimes doubling back in our tracks, as if to surprise a cunning quarry who had somehow evaded our passing.

In each room we encountered one of Brick's sentinels, dour, unsmiling men in the main, who conveyed by their watchful silence the countryman's antipathy toward strangers. In due course we came into Mrs Vincent's own sitting-room, one side of which gave by means of a curtained aperture on to a deep alcove, every face of which was hung in material of a deep burgundy colour.

Our entry was accompanied by the tinkle of tiny bells, and looking up I saw suspended a spray of them so delicately arranged that their gentle welcome continued in response to our slightest movement. As we penetrated the scented atmosphere of the alcove, our feet sank into the pile of a carpet that so exactly matched the hue of the walls that it was difficult to determine where the adjacent planes coincided. The ceiling by contrast was of white plaster, broken only by a single globe illumined by a moderately incandescent gas mantle. At the end of the alcove, centrally placed, stood a good-size mahogany table, with three legs and a round top. One of the legs was thrust toward us, like the tip of an arrow, and there was beyond it nothing but the uninterrupted richness of the Wilton, while on top of the table there reposed on an ebony plinth a large crystal sphere.

All of this was confirmed in the most brilliant detail when Roscoe Brick reached up and pulled the gas lanyard, so flooding the place with light. I saw, too, that there was on the table, in the shadow of the plinth, a lady's vinaigrette, with its stopper removed.

"I was not aware, Mrs Vincent," challenged Sherlock Holmes, "that you are a devotee of the occult?"

"I am interested in the subject," she agreed, averting her eyes, as much, I thought, from my friend's scrutiny as from the strong light. "But I no longer indulge my interest."

"Why not, pray?"

"When Barth - when my dear husband was taken away I looked into the crystal each succeeding day, often for hours on end. But there was nothing, Mr Holmes. The face of the crystal remained blind."

At which juncture the Inspector regulated the gas jet to its original level, and raising his voice above the tintinnabulation his action had made more sonorous said, "I trust that you do not in any way condone this crystal-gazing nonsense, Mr Holmes?"

"Evidently you are not among those who believe that the crystal has an inner eye?"

"Well, you won't catch me sneaking back in here to see what has become of Mr Bartholomew Vincent, if that is what you mean. But play the game! You have not said what is your view of such baubles?"

"My philosophy is well put by the Prince of Denmark, in his address to Horatio on the subject of Heaven and Earth. In the prevailing circumstances, therefore, as the missing banker cannot yet be presumed to be in the first of these two places, I shall confine my investigations to the second, albeit on a somewhat more scientific basis that a mere trooping out of one room and into another. Tut-tut!" prompted Holmes, when the discomfited official made no reply. "Concede that you have proved to your own satisfaction that the fugitive is nowhere in the house?" And when Brick grudgingly did so, "Then *ipso facto* he is somewhere else."

"Well, of course, he is!" exploded the other, smiting his thigh with his cap. "But *where* is he?

"Should you care to join Doctor Watson and me on a

little expedition tomorrow, we shall look into one or two interesting possibilities. Come, Watson, if Mrs Vincent will excuse us I think that we should have an early night. I have every expectation that the morning will prove an energetic and eventful one."

II

"There are those elements in this affair," declared Sherlock Holmes, when we had breakfasted and set off together, "that in their own way present a challenge every bit as formidable as that which confronted Jessop and Telford when they threw the Welsh Canal across the Ceiriog and then drove it under the hill beyond (6).

"Depend upon it, Watson," he continued, as we descended from Krihc House toward the captive band of water and the great man-made structures that contained it, "what we are engaged upon is by no means the humdrum game of hide-and-seek that our friend Brick supposes, although the solution to Mr Bartholomew Vincent's where-abouts is in itself absurdly simple."

"Great Scott, Holmes!" said I, endeavouring to keep pace with his long strides. "Then it is your duty to communicate it to the police."

"As usual, Watson, you have misconceived the essence of the problem. It is not a matter of *cherchez l'homme*, but of arriving at the verities. No, no, my dear fellow, I shall tell no one, least of all the constabulary."

So saying, Mr Sherlock Holmes gained the canal towing path and pointed with his stick to where the waterway constricted before continuing in the form of a narrow channel. "This way," he called, over his shoulder. "If we are to explore Chirk Tunnel, we must first negotiate the aqueduct. Ha! and who better to direct us than Inspector Roscoe Brick?"

The rail viaduct and the canal aqueduct at Chirk.

"Good morning, gentlemen," the police official greeted us. "I fear that there is some repair work in progress inside the tunnel, and that it is impossible to use the towing path."

"How long has this been the case?" demanded Holmes.

"A little over a week."

"Is the waterway closed also?"

"No, but the men must work the boats through and take the horses over the top."

"And where is the police cordon disposed?"

"On the Whitehouses side of the tunnel, but the boats are examined at this end, where it is more convenient. Look! there are two of my officers at the winding hole." (7)

"And does the waterguard supervise vessels plying in either direction?"

"Bless you, no, Mr Holmes! What would be the use of stopping them coming from the Welsh side? It would suppose our man boarding outside the cordon. Downstream, the navigation is patrolled all the way between here and the locks at New Marton."

"That is most illuminating," remarked Sherlock Holmes stooping to pluck some few blades of grass, which he cast upon the water. "It appears there is a slight current at work."

"There is no magic in that, Mr Holmes," laughed Roscoe Brick, with a sly glance in my direction. "The feed is from the Dee, above Llantisilio, and as the water enters strongly and in some volume there is a distinct flow resulting."

"Thank you. What you have said may prove material to my inquiries. Now, as to the railway - my friend indicated the looming presence of the stone viaduct that carried the permanent way alongside the aqueduct, though at a some-what higher elevation - is it likewise patrolled?"

"We keep an eye on it, naturally, and the train crews have been alerted."

"Most commendable. You seem to have catered for every eventuality. And now, if you please, I should like to follow the line of Chirk Tunnel from above ground."

It was a stiff climb that we embarked upon, and one that was made more arduous by the recent very heavy rains, which had so penetrated the surface that our progress dislodged the turf and had us slipping and sliding in muddy gouges of our own making. And yet it was in its way an exhilarating experience, for as we proceeded and our exertions raised us above the great commercial undertakings, these same creations of iron and stone receded into a softer, not unpleasing remoteness. Soon they were gone altogether from our view, and our attention was held instead by a dome-shaped oval stone set nearly flush with the surrounding surface. It measured perhaps a yard and a half in one direction and somewhat less in the other, and I took it to be the cap to some sort of shaft serving the tunnel beneath our feet, a supposition the local man sarcastically confirmed." (8)

"Surely you do not suppose that the fugitive has gained the canal by that route? Unless, of course, he has contrived to raise the stone with his bare hands, and has then somehow set it back in place above his head!"

"Nevertheless, Inspector," replied Sherlock Holmes suavely, "there are at least four ways in which the wanted man might have reached the waterway undetected. Perhaps you would care to consider just one of them?"

"By all means," smiled Brick. "Where do we begin?"

"At either end of Chirk Tunnel, at whose portals the horses pulling the boats are unharnessed. Who would normally bring them over the top?"

"A member of the crew, naturally. A boy, if there is one."

"And if a man and a boy were seen to perform the task? It would appear innocent of deceit, would it not?"

"If two finished what two began."

"Who is to say otherwise? The same constable cannot be in two places at once."

"There is something in what you say, Mr Holmes. From what we know of him, Mr Bartholomew Vincent is a small, spare man, and nimble; with a tarpaulin over his head and a clay pipe stuck between his teeth, he could pass unremarked. Oh, dear, oh, dear, I do believe he could."

It was plain that the man was on tenterhooks, and had what we were about been of a less serious nature his agitated shifting from one foot to the other must have seemed mildly entertaining. "If the rascal has legged it into Inspector Lloyd Williams's domain," he lamented, "I shall be the laughing stock of all Shropshire."

"If what has been conjectured thus far is true," commented Sherlock Holmes, "it follows that in all probability the journey should have proceeded southwards, into England."

"Oh, and why should that be the case?"

"Because it is the line of least resistance. It is also the direction in which craft coming from the Welsh side are not examined."

"By Jove! With the natural drift of water in its favour a well-handled boat would soon make itself scarce. So he is on my ground, after all! I am very much obliged to you, Mr Holmes."

And Police Inspector Roscoe Brick went striding off the way we had come, his sturdy, gaitered figure disappearing into the overcast.

"You have given Brick new hope and purpose," I told Holmes, as we made our own way down. "When you revealed that the fugitive had been transported into England, his sense of relief was greater than his chagrin at being out-smarted."

"And his impetuosity is greater than either. It may appear to him - as it no doubt does to you, Watson - that I have just now postulated an account of Mr Bartholomew Vincent's recent actions, whereas I furnished no more than a logical conclusion to an hypothesis propounded for the Inspector's consideration. I did not say that Vincent had escaped by water, or that he had personated a boatman. It was Brick himself who vivified the phantom and sped it on its way. But we are arrived at Krihc House, where, if I am not in error, we shall shortly see an end to this pantomime."

But not without some plain speaking, for no sooner had we been admitted to the house than Holmes was in contention with its mistress. "If your sole purpose in this business is to secure the freedom of your husband," he began, throwing open the sitting-room door, "you have by your methods embarked upon a most perilous undertaking, and one that is unlikely to succeed. Watson, please have the goodness to pull back that curtain. Ha! The vinaigrette has been displaced a fraction to the left, I fancy, while the plinth supporting the crystal is perhaps a trifle nearer the front of the table."

I was of the opinion that all within the alcove was exactly as before, even to the delicately perfumed atmosphere and the sound of bells.

"You are quite right in supposing that my one concern is for the liberty of my husband," declared Mrs Shelagh Vincent, compelling by her manner our complete attention. "Not, you understand, for the false liberty of a man on the run, but for the true liberty of one who is declared free."

"Then why, pray, did you not make these unequivocal representations to me when you came to Baker Street, instead of trading upon your paternal name to command my interest?"

"Do you mean to say that had I come with no more than a plea to reopen Bartholomew's case you would have listened to me? Or truly given the weight of your consideration to the plight of a good and honourable man? I think not, Mr Holmes. It was only by revealing that I am the sister of Professor James Moriarty that I could hope to persuade you to visit Krihc House, here to see for yourself that the hunt for my husband is conducted with inhuman zeal."

"That much at least is true," replied Holmes. And then, in a harsher tone of voice: "And what did you hope to gain by perpetuating the riddle of your husband's hiding place?"

"Time in which to convince you of my sincerity."

"Are you quite certain that you did not intend that I, too, should be baffled as to his whereabouts?"

"Quite certain."

"Or that I should be instrumental in dispatching Inspector Roscoe Brick on a wild goose chase?"

"You must believe what you will."

"And how could you know that I should solve the riddle? Or that, were I to do so, I should not broadcast the solution to the world at large?"

"Because you are Sherlock Holmes," whispered Mrs Vincent. "Our future is in your hands," she added, in a stronger voice. "I care nothing for myself, but in pity's name tell me what you intend?"

"My intention," returned Holmes, in ringing tones, "is to make it known that as a deposit of good faith prior to my testing the evidence presented at the trial of Mr Bartholomew Vincent, the said Bartholomew Vincent shall within the hour surrender himself into the custody of the police.

"It will be as well," he appended, in an aside to the silent woman, "if he were to do so at some point in the vicinity of the Welsh Canal, and thus vindicate to that extent the professional judgement of Inspector Brick. Those are my terms, Madam. Come, Watson! It is time we were getting on our way."

"Mrs Shelagh Moriarty Vincent is indeed a most remarkable woman," resumed Holmes, as the fly bore us toward the railway station. "Let us hope that her faith in her husband is not misplaced."

"You have not yet said where the banker is hid," I reminded him.

"Oh, I should have thought that it is obvious."

"Not to me, Holmes."

"Then I shall enlighten you. What do you know of the angles of incidence and reflection?"

"That they are to do with the behaviour of light when directed at a reflective surface, and that they are always equal."

"Just so, Watson ..."

Now the fly was setting us down at the railway station, and it was not for some time, when we were installed in the relative comfort of a first-class smoking-compartment and were rattling through the pleasant Shropshire countryside, that Sherlock Holmes chose to develop his theme.

Then he described in the most vivid detail an astonishing feat of magic he had once witnessed, when there was presented to the audience an open-fronted cubicle the size of a small room, each inside surface of which was clad in green baize. The single item of furniture within this monochromatic enclosure was a small table having three legs and a round top.

"At this point," continued Holmes, drawing contentedly at the pipe he had just now lighted, "there appeared on the stage a fellow carrying an ebony box.

"'I am recently returned from Egypt'," he announced, setting down the box in the centre of the table, 'where I acquired this remarkable artefact. Are you there, Sphinx?' he called, tapping the top of the box.

"'I am present, O Master,' came a muffled response; whereupon the magician threw open the front of the box to reveal the head of a Sphinx.

"'Awake, Sphinx!' he commanded. And, as the creature stirred and opened its eyes, 'Can you solve the riddles of the Universe?'

"'I can and I will, O Master. Ask and it shall be made known.'

"The magician now put to the Sphinx a number of questions, to which it gave prompt, if enigmatic, replies. Eventually its inquisitor saluted the Sphinx, then closed the door of the box.

"'Ashes to ashes, dust to dust', he intoned, and re-opening the door demonstrated that the space beyond was empty save a small heap of dust (9).

"I perceive, Watson, that you do not share the astonishment of the magician's audience," probed Sherlock Holmes, regarding me through a swirl of tobacco smoke. "Possibly you are of the opinion that the inscrutability of the Sphinx was penetrated by other than supernatural means?"

"By ventriloquism," said I.

"By no means," said he. "The magician was at times on the far side of the stage when the Sphinx spoke out."

"Some sort of mechanical device."

"The lips moved in perfect harmony."

"An accomplice, then."

"One that did not possess a body, it seems!" My friend's thin lips curved in an amused smile. "Nevertheless, you are on the right track, and one that leads undeniably from a harmless entertainment to the altogether more desperate deception practised by Mr and Mrs Bartholomew Vincent."

Holmes smoked in silence for a while, and then said matter of factly: "The convict husband hid beneath the table in the alcove whenever danger threatened. We know from Inspector Roscoe Brick's description that Vincent is a small man and agile. Oh, come now, Watson, it is elementary, surely, that the mirrors occupying the two appearing sides of the table would, when viewed from the entrance to the alcove, reflect their surroundings and the space beneath the table appear to be empty." (10)

"By Jove, Homes!" I cried, grasping at last the scientific principles upon which the illusion depended. "I see it all now!"

"Do you indeed? Then perhaps you will be so good as to continue in my stead? It is evident that to you the riddle of Krihc House is a riddle no longer."

"Sorry, Holmes," I murmured, mindful how stiff he can become when he considers an interjection in any way pejorative to his orderly unravelling of a case. "I was merely about to remark how clever of Mrs Vincent it was to substitute for the ebony box a plinth and crystal."

"Just so," he agreed, somewhat mollified. "Although they served quite different ends. In the public instance the box was used to cover a trap-door in the top of the table, while at Krihc House the crystal was used to suggest that the alcove was a retreat for a sad and gullible woman. You recognize, of course, the purpose of the bells depending from the ceiling?"

Without awaiting my reply, Holmes went on to draw an unexpected parallel between our present location and the *mise en scène* at the house. "Believe me, Watson, given the most singular circumstances in which it was employed that simple device was capable of signalling danger every bit as effectively as would be the pulling of the communication handle above our heads."

"And the purpose of the vinaigrette?"

"There are two ways of recognizing a recent gaol-bird, Watson. One is by his pallor; the other is by the odour that attends his person. The purpose of the vinaigrette was to mask by its aromatic emissions the proximity of a fugitive."

Now that Holmes had revealed the sanctuary at Krihc House, I appreciated how discretely at its farthermost end had been situate the innocent-looking table, how readily the clappers in the bells had responded to the slightest stimulus, and how pervasive had been the aroma issuing from the unstoppered vinaigrette. Of the five perceptive senses, three had been catered for in the most ingenious way. It had taken the unique deductive powers of Sherlock Holmes to see beyond the superficialities, and the remarkable intuitive gift of Mrs Shelagh Moriarty Vincent to divine that he would do so.

For some few miles of our journey Holmes and I maintained a companionable silence, and it was not until our carriage was being pulled swaying and jolting over the points outside Shrewsbury that I broached those aspects of the case that still baffled me.

"You decreed that Mr Bartholomew Vincent must surrender himself to the police if you are to inquire into the circumstances leading to his conviction for embezzlement: do you consider that his wife will acquaint him with your ultimatum?"

"I am certain that she will not."

"Because he will not heed her?"

"Because he does not need twice telling, Watson. Why do you suppose I spoke so loudly at our little confabulation in the alcove, if not to put Vincent himself in no doubt as to the condition?"

"He was beneath the table even then?"

"He dare not be otherwise."

"Will he act in concert with your wishes?"

"I do not doubt it. Indeed, it appears that the news has preceded us. Look, Watson! There on the station placard!"

Following with my eyes the direction of his extended finger, I was in time to glimpse through a crowd of excited bystanders the crayoned words ESCAPED CONVICT TAKEN.

"Our friend Brick is no doubt the hero of the hour,"

137

laughed Sherlock Holmes, reaching down his travelling bag, "and is seen by his superiors as the man who brought a perplexing case to a timely end. But come along, my dear fellow," he added briskly, throwing open the compartment door. "If we are to keep our part of the bargain, it will be necessary to put up in Shrewsbury for a few days."

Footnotes

(1) Shropshire does not appear in the canonical writings, though Holmes and Watson came near when they visited the neighbouring county of Hereford, in connection with the Boscombe Valley case.

(2) It has not hitherto been mooted that the Moriarty siblings extended beyond the three brothers: Professor James Moriarty; Colonel James (*sic*) Moriarty; and he who was a station-master in the West of England.

(3) Becoming Clwyd in the Local Government Act of 1972.

(4) Until about the middle of 1910 there was out of Paddington a train at 11.25 am, connecting at Shrewsbury with a local train that reached Chirk at 4.02 pm. After this date, when the Bicester cut-off came into use, the departure time from Paddington and the arrival time at Chirk became 11.05 am and 3.28 pm respectively.

(5) That it was sufficiently dark suggests that Holmes's party reached Chirk by the later of the two trains postulated in Note (4); that is, at 4.02 pm, and on a gloomy day in December. It follows that the journey took place sometime prior to the middle of 1910 (when the schedules changed), and in any case not later than December, 1909. The hypothesis fails, however, if it can be shown that the trio caught the earlier train and that it ran, say, half an hour late.

(6) From 1801 an aqueduct carried the canal in a cast iron trough 70 feet" above the River Ceiriog.

(7) Whitehouses is at the north (Welsh) end of Chirk Tunnel. The winding hole (a widening of the cut where boats may be turned) is situated between the north end of the aqueduct and the south end of the tunnel.

8) The inspection shaft is located central to the tunnel gauge, with its longer axis in the tunnel line, and is approximately 305 yards from the south portal, the tunnel length between portals being 495 yards.

(9) In 1865 there appeared at the Egyptian Hall, Piccadilly, an illusionist calling himself Colonel Stodare, who presented 'an astonishing feat of magic' exactly as Holmes describes.

(10) The understructure of the table was essentially a triangular prism, the third (back-facing) side remaining open to permit entry and exit.

ACKNOWLEDGEMENTS

The photographs reproduced in this book apparently reached Doctor John Watson from divers sources, and fragmentary references found among his effects indicate that, as well as to him, the publishers should extend their thanks and acknowledgements to the following:

Lancashire County Library
(specifically the libraries of Burnley, Clitheroe, and Preston)

Manchester City Libraries

Shropshire County Library
(specifically the library of Shrewsbury)

Douglas R P Ferriday
(The Douglas R P Ferriday Collection)

Watkins of Ripon

If, inadvertently, further courtesies are due but not recorded, the publishers as well as extending their apologies plead the lack of data among the good Doctor's papers.